THE COVID

COLENSO BOOKS
WILL DONATE ANY PROFITS
FROM THE SALE OF THIS BOOK
TO CHARITIES WHICH BENEFIT
THE UK NATIONAL HEALTH SERVICE
AND ITS STAFF . . .

THE NHS STAFF
TO WHOM THIS BOOK
IS DEDICATED
IN GRATITUDE
FOR THEIR
EXTRAORDINARY
DEVOTION
IN THE FACE
OF INCOMPARABLE
DIFFICULTIES

Contributors
of poetry, prose and pictures

MARK ALLEN

SUZIE BLACK

ADRIANNA GOMEZ DANGREMOND

SARAH EKDAWI

ELIZABETH ELLIS

ISABEL FIELD REID

SUE FIELD REID

LILY FLINTOFF

FRANCES HASTE

POLLY HASTE

ANTHONY HIRST

BRIAN JAGGER

DI JAGGER

CECILIA LOULAKAKI-MOORE

IRENE LOULAKAKI-MOORE

WILF LUNN

WILLIAM MERRETT

FAYSAL MIKDADI

JULIAN NANGLE

JIM POTTS

NINA-MARIA POTTS

ALICE RAINEY

MARIA STRANI-POTTS

ALBIE WADDELL

OTIS WADDELL

SUSAN WALPOLE

IAN WHITWHAM

The

Covid Years

a composite journal

from many hands

in poetry,

prose and pictures

designed and edited by

Anthony Hirst

COLENSO BOOKS
2023

First published November 2023 by
Colenso Books
68 Palatine Road, London N16 8ST
colensobooks@gmail.com

ISBN 978-1-912788-30-9

"Dodona Oracle", "Prika" and "Corfu" were first published
in Jim Potts, *Corfu Blues* (Stockholm: Ars Interpres Publications, 2006)

"Dodona Oracle", "Taken short" and "Prika" were previously published in
Jim Potts, *Reading the Signs* (London: Colenso Book, 2020)

"Generation or Gender" was first published in Anthony Hirst, *Flora and fauna
(hominids included)* (Birmingham: Delos Press, 2021).

"The bench", "The Devil's Advocate and the Coronavirus Pandemic",
"Grim Prospects — autumnal Monday", "Brave cowards" and "Corfu"
were previously published in Jim Potts, *Words on the table*
(London: Colenso books, 2021).

"This magical rain" by Julian Nangle, and "Maria, swimming" and "The key"
by Jim Potts were first published in *TOPM (The Occasional Poetry Magazine)*,
31 October 2022 (Dorchester: The Occasional Bookshop)
and are included here by agreement with Julian Nangle.

The image on page 45 is reproduced by permission of Frazer Muggeridge Studio.

The image on page 90 is reproduced by permission of The Stilltime Collection.

Poems by those still under 18 at the date of publication are published by
permission of their parents as follows:

"Life" by Albie Waddell and "It's not a monster" (painting) by Otis Waddell
are published by permission of Polly Haste and Nicholas Waddell.

"I Miss You Guys" by William Merrett
is published by permission of Diane and Richard Merrett.

"Holding on to letting go", "In the left pocket of your leather jacket" and
"Counting" by Lily Flintoff are published
by permission of Elaine Gay and Crispin Flintoff.

Although aged 15 at the time of writing "A Viral Vision",
Cecilia Loulakaki-Moore is over 18 at the date of publication.

The photo on the front cover shows an intermediate stage in the accretion
of graffiti on a Covid poster in a small park, Butterfield Green,
Stoke Newington, London N16. Photos of the other stages can
be found with the poem "Mass Psychosis?" on pages 161–164.

CONTENTS

KEY TO CONTRIBUTORS

Titles of images are in SMALL CAPITALS; where they are also in quotation marks, they are not titles as such, but words present within the image. Items marked with an asterisk in the period March 15th to May 20th, 2020 (and one item now placed later), were first published in *Viral Verse: pandemic poems and images* (June 2020). A long dash (————) in the sequence of dates indicates either that the item is undated or that its date is not part of the chronological sequence. Where the ages of under-eighteens are given, here and on the pages where their contributions appear, they are their ages at the time of writing or creating.

A COMPOSITE JOURNAL IN POETRY, PROSE AND PICTURES
2020

CONTENTS

(2020)

(2020)

(2020)

Continued over . . .

2021

IN MEMORIAM FAYSAL MIKDADI

———— o ————

(2021)

2022

THE SEA AND MARIA

(A MEMORIAL TRIBUTE TO MARIA STRANI-POTTS)

———— o ————

(2022)

2023

————— o —————

EDITOR'S INTRODUCTION

This book was originally intended to be a sequel to *Viral Verse: Pandemic poems and images*, published in June 2020, and containing contributions dating from March 22nd to May 20th of that first year of Covid. But in the interests of presenting the Covid period from March 2020 to January 2023 as a whole it was decided that all of the material in *Viral Verse* should be included in the present volume. Nothing has been omitted except the "Selective timeline of the Covid-19 Pandemic in the UK and USA". This took up three full pages to cover the first four months from mid January to mid May 2020 and its extension through another two years and eight months would have created something far too cumbersome. Many of the details matter less with the passage of time and the sequence of the contributions themselves tells, I think, enough of the public story; besides, extensive timelines of the pandemic can easily be found now on the Internet.

Many of the sixteen contributors to *Viral Verse* have sent me additional poems, prose pieces and pictures (photographs or artwork) for the present volume, and contributions were received from eleven other people who were not represented in *Viral Verse*, thus there are twenty-seven contributors to *The Covid Years*. Most of the contributors were in the UK throughout this strange period, though there are contributions from France, Greece, Italy and the USA. In age the contributors ranged from seven to over eighty at the time of writing or producing artwork.

In *The Covid Years* the arrangement of the written contributions is more strictly chronological than in *Viral Verse*, in line with the idea of a journal. This means that the poems taken over from *Viral Verse* have been partially rearranged and new poems and prose pieces which are dated within the time frame of the earlier volume have been inserted among them. The position of visual material is not in most cases determined by its date.

There are exceptions to the strict chronological arrangement of the written material. There are two groups of poems in this book which constitute memorial tributes to two of the contributors, Faysal Mikdadi who died in August 2021, and Maria

Strani-Potts who died in May 2022, and the position of these groups is determined by a single poem within each group.

The tribute to Faysal begins with his own last contribution to this volume, dated February 2nd, 2021, but the poems in mourning for Faysal which follow were, obviously, written after his death and one of them as late as the beginning of 2022, but it is the poem by Faysal himself which determines the position of the tribute in this book.

In the section entitled "The Sea and Maria" the poems by Maria's husband, Jim Potts, cover a long period, from 1968 to April 2023. His latest poem, "The Globe and the Plaque" was added when the book was in the final stages of preparation, together with extracts from the "Epilogue" to Maria's unpublished autobiography, and the reflections of her daughter on the first anniversary of Maria's death. The position of the tribute in the sequence is determined by the date ("Late May, 2022") of Jim's "Miroloyi for Maria — a lament", the first poem that he wrote after her death.

Two Prologues precede the chronologically arranged "composite journal": a selection of haiku by the seventeenth-century Japanese poet Bashō, and a funeral poem by contributor Mark Allen, which he wrote before Covid, in 2016. The reasons for the inclusion of these prologues are given on pages 1 and 5.

I could say that I am sorry that my own contributions take up so much space, but it might make more sense to say I regret that I did not receive more contributions from other people. In terms of numbers of contributions I am closely followed by Jim Potts. I would like to thank Jim here not only for the numerous poems and photographs that he contributed, but for his support and encouragement throughout this project and for being the intermediary who brought in a number of the other contributors.

My thanks to everyone for their contributions, for their patience in answering my questions and for their patience more generally in waiting such a long time for this book to finally see the light of day.

Anthony Hirst, October 2023

Prologue

from the distant Past

1666 – 1694

In these haiku from three-and-a-half centuries ago and half-a-world away, there are many pre-echoes of moods, sentiments, circumstances, and even phrases to be found in the poems of very recent years that follow.

Haiku of isolation and sorrow

by Matsuo Bashō (b. 1644, d. 1694)

In my native place,
over my birth-cord I weep,
the year almost gone.

       This the year's first day.
       Time to feel the loneliness
       of autumn's passing.

Locked in by winter
again, I'll nestle against
this old post of mine.

       Brought down low — the world
       upside down and out of joint.
       Snow's seized the bamboo.

Like clouds we part, friend,
for a time, but like wild geese
we'll live to return.

       A weathered skeleton
       my mind shows me, as the wind
       bites into my flesh.

However well-stoked,
a fire can be extinguished
by the *ssss* of tears.

All manner of things
come back into my mind here
by this cherry tree.

Now spring is leaving,
birds are weeping, and fishes'
eyes are full of tears.

Briefly, by the falls,
I am alone — my summer
retreat begins here.

So much summer grass.
So many warriors' dreams.
This is where they lie.

Would that gravemound could be
removed by my tearful voice
in the autumn wind.

An autumn wind blows
yet Ise's graveyards can feel
even more lonely.

Won't you turn this way?
Like you I too am lonely
this autumn evening.

All these sad notches.
Bamboo shoots — to become one
is each person's end.

Feeling sad before,
how lonely now it makes me feel —
this common cuckoo.

> All these hydrangeas —
> a thicket for this garden's
> solitary house.

At these ears of wheat
for support I thought to clutch
at time of parting.

> No one's a number —
> don't think of yourself like that
> on these days of souls.

I am on a road
no other person travels
in the autumn night.

> In such an autumn
> why must one grow old? — A bird
> heading for the clouds.

Travelling and sick,
my dreams on an arid plain
run round in circles.

English versions of the haiku, AH,
selected from Bashō Redistilled (a work in progress)

Prologue

from the recent past

2016

The following poem by Mark Allen, who has contributed two other poems to this book, does not belong to the Covid Years. It is a funeral oration in verse for a life that lasted less than an hour. It has been included because it will touch the hearts of many who lost children during the Covid years.

In memory of Thomas

We may never know
what shocking fate
crushed tiny Thomas
after so short a time;
what made life seem
so fragile and so precious.
We may never know.

We will never know
how tiny Thomas would have
bonded with Jack his twin,
how they would have played,
cried and laughed.
Just like his father Tom
and his soul mate James.
The coming together of two
generations of identical beings,
explaining the past
and shaping the future.
We will never know.

We will never know
what might have been.
When — not if — Thomas would
have plucked his first guitar.
Whether he would have an angel's
voice, like his mother Sophie.
Whether he would have picked
sentences from Latin prose,
or traded a cricket bat

for an arts' degree.
We will never know.

We will never know
what might have been.
But let our imaginations
play havoc with our despair.
Just picture Thomas at 22,
enjoying a special celebration.
He is tall and handsome,
like his father Tom.
He has just graduated or
played his first main gig.
He is surrounded by friends
and he is laughing and joking,
enjoying the moment, his
friends hanging on every word.
You can see his parents
and grandparents
pumped with pride, greedily
grabbing this special moment.
And this is one of many memories
we will never know.

We will never know
what cruel meaning there is
to grief, but we think of Lear.
"As flies to wanton boys are
we to the gods. They kill us
For their sport."
And we try to make sense of this
topsy-turvy nonsense world.
We will never know.

We will never know
why, but we do know this.
Thomas lived for 48 minutes
and died in his father's arms.
For 48 precious minutes
Thomas was enmeshed in love.
We, his parents and family,
will always treasure him.
We will never know
the answers to our questions.
But Jack lives on and so
does our love for tiny Thomas.

The Covid Years

a composite journal

from many hands

in poetry, prose and pictures

March 2020 – January 2023

Social distancing

Detail from an ipad painting by SFR which appeared in colour on the front cover of Viral Verse: Pandemic poems and images. The full painting is shown opposite.

Report from Mondaino
(Province of Rimini, Emilia-Romagna, Italy)

Life extremely awkward here. *Everything* closed since last Monday. Such silence. Makes you go mad. Much much worse for people in blocks of flats with children of course. Even dog-walking is limited to ten minutes a day and if you meet anyone you should cross the road. We have land, thank God.

Illegal to leave Mondaino. Have seen no-one except Basil who delivers food etc. every few days. No sign of future changes. Iris in another province so cannot visit. She is holed up in a horrible flat with a six-month old baby too.

And obviously all bookings cancelling so we will earn no money this year. Very worrying situation indeed.

Sunday March 15th, 2020, SB in an email to SFR

(Basil and Iris are the writer's son and daughter)

London Euston to Manchester Piccadilly
on the Covid-19 Express
(a journey to a funeral)

Cold spring sunshine.
The train goes past a long, smooth lake.
Some twenty swans.
Next a pub, THE PRETTY PIGS.

Nine coaches.
Three or four of us in each.
Well spread out, as instructed.
Hazards to each other.

Most trees still winter-naked.
Broad, flat, half-flooded, empty fields.
Fresh habitats
for water fowl.

Whole fields of solar panels.
Mounted at a low angle.
Signs of hope
for an infected world?

A few solitary daffodils
amongst the scrub
on the steep bank
of a railway cutting.

A canal.
A long line of tethered barges.
Black-and-white cattle grazing.
No sign of bipeds.

The first stop, Crewe.
"Oh, Mister Porter,
whatever shall I do?"
— when nothing makes sense anymore.

"Please make sure
you take all your luggage
and belongings with you."
But the sense of belonging's gone.

"And please mind the step
down to the platform."
Yes, we're all stepping down.
Or are we stepping off . . . ?

On the platform there's
THE CALM CORNER.
Door locked, though. A room
where we might sit too close together.

Manchester. The suburbs.
Empty streets. The station
almost deserted,
barriers all open.

On to Huddersfield.
TRANSPENNINE.
Stan'edge — we're entering
one of the UK's longest tunnels . . .

March 22nd, 2020, AH

The Great Field, Poundbury

*The Great Field provides 12 hectares
of green space for the residents of
Dorchester, with more than 26,000
shrubs and 450 trees planted.*
                    DUCHY OF CORNWALL

On the first day of Lockdown,
they cancelled my lung scan.
I was relieved —
but postponed for how long?
I could not have believed
things could happen so fast.
In spite of the ban, I walked and I ran
amongst young budding trees
all recently planted
around the Great Field,
now empty of people.

The saplings give hope,
seem to say Spring is here
but how long must we wait?

I head back for home
and *hyper*-hyperventilate.

March 23rd, 2020, JP
(Sequel: May 3rd, 2020, page 53)

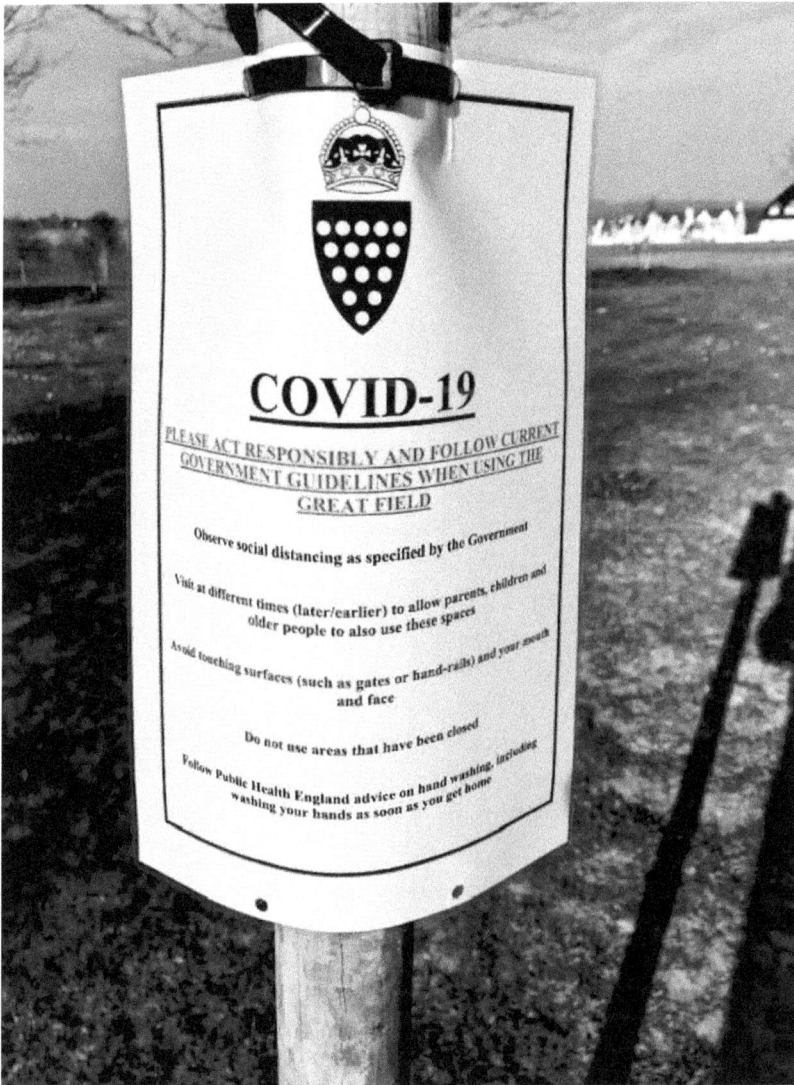

COVID-19

PLEASE ACT RESPONSIBLY AND FOLLOW CURRENT GOVERNMENT GUIDELINES WHEN USING THE GREAT FIELD

Observe social distancing as specified by the Government

Visit at different times (later/earlier) to allow parents, children and older people to also use these spaces

Avoid touching surfaces (such as gates or hand-rails) and your mouth and face

Do not use areas that have been closed

Follow Public Health England advice on hand washing, including washing your hands as soon as you get home

This notice went up around the beginning of April 2020.

Photo: April 11th, 2020, MSP

In brief

The streets are empty.
Seclusion has gone viral.
The sky is silent.

March 24th, 2020, AH

Donald's "beautiful timeline"

Sunak's in his counting house
    counting out your money.
Johnson's locked in Number Ten
    feeling rather funny.

The Last Trump's in the White House
    blowing his own trumpet
and wondering what this thing can be
    if trumpery can't trump it.

He'd like to see Death done to death
    at least by Easter Sunday.
If Jesus did it, so can he —
    he'll be Messiah — *one* day!

March 25th, 2020, AH

Disjunction

It's spring — and nature's waking up again.
    But, out of step, as ever,
the human race goes into hibernation.

March 26th, 2020, AH

Lockdown Snapshot

Another day of nothing
but motor round the block,
slow travelling as older people do
(when they can).
She caught us looking at her
from our car into her front room.

Dressed for the day
all beige and grey and gloom.

As if she were a song, paused.
One hand on her neck. Uncertainty.
Although there are few Covid
cases up North, as yet.

I don't know what
she thought of us
peering in her window
as one would study a leaning fish
wavering off course a bit.

March 26, 2020, AR

Lockdown UK-style Week 1

Strange, this quiet urban world we now inhabit.
My almost daily outings in the bright
spring sunlight to get food, *The Guardian*,
from one or other local shop or petrol
station; and some exercise — some days extended
to the less-local post office with packages
of books to keep my online business going.

Strange, passing so few people in the streets,
but every passing now more memorable
than in the past. We move aside, the stranger
and I, to put two-metres' space between us
as we pass; or else one may stand aside,
in a shop doorway or behind a lamppost,
or step right off into the road
to let the other, or the others, pass.
I try to catch their eyes, a half-formed smile
ready on my lips, which, if our eyes meet,
becomes a little broader. Some smile in return,
acknowledging a wistful sort of sympathy.
Words may be exchanged: "Hi", "Hello",
"Good morning" or "Good afternoon"
. . . and strangers have become less strange.

Those wearing masks have only eyes to smile with.
And quite a few are wrapped up in their fear,
stare resolutely at the ground or turn their heads,
avoiding even catching sight of the other
dangerous creatures who roam the streets.

March 26th, 2020, AH

Covidity and other
terms of reference

A-vid-ity: the wilful blindness of the super-rich.

Cupidity: what got them there — the theft
of "surplus value" that was never surplus
    in the blighted lives of others.

Stupidity means fit to rule the world.

Acidity: the aftertaste of lies.

Placidity means doing nothing UK/US style
    until it's far too late.

Morbidity (increasing exponentially):
    your chances of not coming through.

Co-vid-ity means seeing things together.
    And perhaps at last we are.

Trump means seeing nothing but your own sweet face
    reflected in a gilt-edged mirror.

Boris means *see it my way* and "Let's get it done!"
    But what "it" means is anybody's guess.

Covidity means seeing things together.
    And maybe, now, we can.

March 28th, 2020, AH

Number games
or
Well done, Mr President

Fauci, the infection expert, has spoken out
and Trump's retuned his trumpet.

Fauci anticipates
between a hundred thousand
and two hundred thousand
Americans will die
even with precautions.

"Horrible number" says the President.
But up his sleeve — luckily for him —
he's got some numbers far more horrible
(just like his syntax): "I kept asking
and we did models . . . These are
two-point-two million people would have died,"
if the US, that is, had tried to "wing it"
— just as Trump did at first.

So Fauci's figures aren't Fake News.
They give the President a let-out clause.
"Too little and too late" will be forgotten,
Trump's action now will save the nation,
with room for reasonable fluctuation
in the figures: "If we could hold that down . . .
to a hundred thousand, maybe even less,
but to a hundred thousand, so we have got
between a hundred and two hundred thousand
we altogether have done
A VERY GOOD JOB." Applause, please.
A triumph for the President.

Since then the White House has carved out
for him a bit more wriggle room:
it's two hundred and forty thousand dead
that's now the upper limit.

Bob Dylan in the Sixties
informed our generation
(his, mine and Trump's, I mean,
if Trump was listening then),

"there's no success like failure"
and with the right PR we'll all forget
that "failure's no success at all".

March 31st, 2020, AH

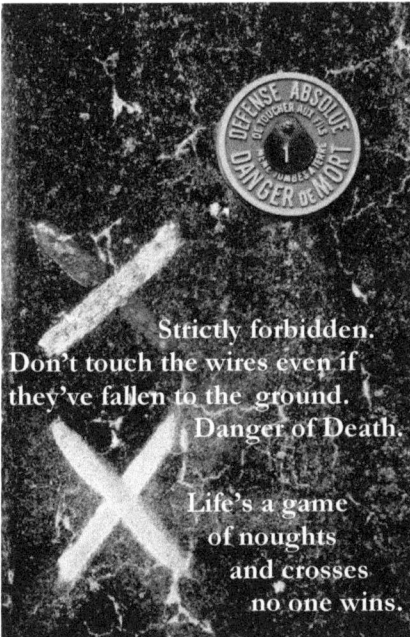

Face of a concrete post for an electric power line, with waymarks for walkers. Bossay-sur-Claise Indre et Loire, France. (Photo, translation of warning and other words: AH)

21

The other Big C

Old lady, selling off
her husband's vinyl:
saving for his headstone.

Hello, Hermes, psychopomp,
thanks for the message:
"Caught Covid — can't fly!"

What a way to end our days,
with colleges closed,
no vaccine in sight.

One bad mistake that God made:
set Covid rolling.
His pinball arcade.

March 31st, 2020, JP

Age-at-death unknown

Now seventy-five, I was aware
that Death was never far away
but also felt he was in no
great hurry or focussed especially
on me. But since he has acquired
another name, Great Covid,
it's clear that Death is never more
than two or three weeks off for anyone
whatever age they are, and that
he has become more arbitr'y than ever,
rejoicing in the empty streets
as evidence of his great power
to terrorize.

      And "power" brings me
to our P.M., aged fifty-five,
who's in intensive care, and, though
I'm far from fond of him, and even think
this land might be a better place
if he had not been born, or else
had never entered politics,
I can't but wish this fellow foolish
human a full recovery
and keep on hold a mocking poem
I wrote that plays games with his name
until he's well and in control
(like Death) again, if Death permit.

April 7th, 2020, AH
(see also pages 46–47)

But is it war?

"It's not the Blitz," some wise heads say.
        Why is it then
the "Covid-Nineteen *War* Cabinet"
        now rules the day?

April 7th, 2020, AH
(see also page 58)

Let us pray — or preferably not

If you don't pray and don't believe —
and in most cases I am sure
in fact you don't — then please stop saying,
you politicians, spokes*men* for this and that
(and mostly you are *men*), that *all*
your *thoughts and PRAYERS are with —*
or *go out to — the families of the victims.*

Hypocrisy and cut-price piety! It stinks —
unless you big-guys are so frightened now
you're calling on a God you don't believe in
        in case you got it wrong.

Perhaps, though, it's the only way you know
to add a touch of that solemnity
you think's required. Grow up. Speak plain.
By all means let us have your "thoughts",
        but STUFF your phoney "prayers".

April 9th, 2020, AH

Silent Springs

In Rachel Carson's *Silent Spring*
it was the birds and insects, hit
by DDT, who'd soon be falling silent.

In Covid-Nineteen's Silent Spring
of Twenty-Twenty, it's the birds'
gigantic noisy man-made counterparts

who've disappeared. The London sky
this sunny April's blue and empty
no longer criss-crossed by their vapour trails.

Heathrow, for now, scarcely has need
of even a single runway — let's forget,
for now, the bitterly contested third.

It's bliss for those of us whose houses lie
beneath the flight paths and the "holding stacks"
— scarcely a daytime minute ever passed

before, without at least one plane in sight,
and within hearing. Often there'd be two
or three together overhead.

April 10th, 2020, AH

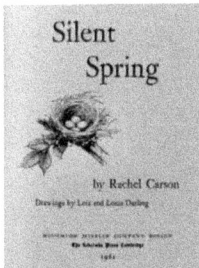

Silent
Spring

by Rachel Carson
Drawings by Lois and Louis Darling

Panic Rap

Panic! Panic! Panic!
And Pandemonium
Her life is one emergency
One long uncertainty
Scans don't lie
No alibi
A lump on the lung
A shadow 'cross the sun
Stage 4 it's a war
Murder on the poison floor
The chemo nearly kills her
Mercy she can't take no more!
Bring on the radiation
Burn the fucker to the bone
The radiation it don't fix a thing
Just a scar upon the skin
Bring on the immunotherapy
The immune it don't make
No one immune
Panic! Panic! Panic!
And Pandemonium
Here comes a pandemic!
Her life's a piece of panic
Covid nineteen
It's a scream
Cut throat stuff
A-tishoo! A-tishoo!
You're going to fall down
A-tishoo A-tishoo!
You're going to drown
Pretty blood red
Wake up dead

She's got no defences
She's going senseless
She's got the co – morbidities
Got those vulnerabilities
Don't want a tracheostomy
Don't want those ventilator blues
So lock her up and lock her down
And throw away the key
Put her under heavy manners
A window's all she'll see
The NHS's a war zone
She's a bag of bones
A soul in a sack
No coming back
Panic! ! Panic! Panic!
It's Pandemonium

April 10th, 2020, IW
(see also pages 31 & 120–121)

Wandering Widsith's
Original Corona Virus Homesick Blues

Widsið maðolade, wordhord onleac . . .
Widsith speaks, unlocks his word-hoard . . .

They call me Wandering Widsith, Widsith is my name, *(twice)*
the way that they mistreat me, it's a low-down crying shame.

I used to be a singer, singing praises for my pay, *(twice)*
now I've got the symptoms, I've got no place to stay.

I've wandered over Europe, with my harp and my word-hoard, *(twice)*
but times are getting hard now, they won't give me bed and board.

They want to lock me up and leave me, that's the way it seems, *(twice)*
to keep me at a distance, so I can't unlock my dreams.

April 12th, 2020, JP

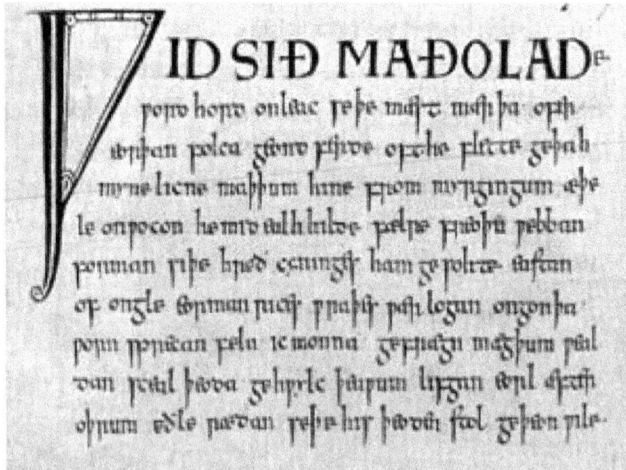

Fourth week

It isn't very long since we
began to isolate, to distance
from our friends,
yet some would say a lifetime passed.

I know that in the future we will
talk about this time —
of friends we missed, of friends now gone
and happy times of love so
quietly pervading home
in many little ways; the look
which passed between us as we
walked through daily life,
the lightest touch on cheek or arm
just telling how we care,
the fleeting kiss and whispered
"I love you" mean so much more
when isolation draws you close,
much closer than before perhaps.

In oh so many ways, my love,
my heart grows fonder still.
I loved you then, I love you now,
I know I always will.
So stand awhile beside me here;
together, we shall face the world.

April 13th, 2020, SW

Empty streets

The streets are beautiful.
And empty.
Not beautiful *because* they're empty
but because it's spring.

Blossom exploding
and new, light foliage.
An aching beauty
because the streets are empty.

Well, not quite,
but there're so few of us
to feel the trees spring back to life
— and so many dying.

The rest locked down
inside their houses,
apart in their apartments,
waiting for life to come back.

April 14th, 2020, AH

! If the Cancer doesn't get you the Corona Virus will !

Standing like an astronaut in the pale and useless sun
Masked and veiled and gelled and pale her life a loaded gun
She totters on unmuscled limbs that could bop until she dropped
That once skipped rope, bent branches, or did the Lindy Hop

If the cancer doesn't get you the corona virus will.

The faceless nurse comes to collect her in the falling light
She's carted off down corridors screened and out of sight
They want more blood to check she can survive those poison cures
They want a scan to see if she can endure that killing floor.

If the cancer doesn't get you the corona virus will

She's smuggled like a rumour through corona corridors
She could catch a death on any breath on those culling floors.
She's whisked out like a whisper half-daft on the morphine,
Fat chance of curing cancer while corona's on the wind

She's lost in a lockdown she stares out of a window
And meditates on blossoms and bending branches in the wind
She meditates on morphine and the splendour in the grass
And sometimes keeps from crying that everything must pass

If the cancer doesn't get you the corona virus will
If the cancer doesn't get you the corona virus will

April 15th, 2020, IW
(see also pages 26–27 and 120–121)

999 call

He turned to admire
pink cherry blossom. But where
is that ambulance?

April 15th, 2020, JP

Photo: April 12th, 2020, IFR

Discharged!

He'd been discharged from the Covid ward
and the threat of that Damocles' sword,
not knowing what fate he might meet
on that wheeled bed with its slippery sheet.

Home for his birthday, out of danger,
still with wristband, still half a stranger,
still with feelings of anger and guilt
mixed with joy in the gift of a quilt.

It covers him now, keeps him warm,
he's safe at home, and out of the storm.
Each patch is a year of his life,
in each stitch the love of his wife.

April 16th, 2020, JP

A Viral Vision

It started with a rumour and spread until it reigned upon Earth . . . This virus bore a crown as it made all of earth's people bow down and obey its tyrant-like appearance. How cruel and bigoted life can be. How strenuous for you to keep up with, yet effortless for it to force you into stagnating in time, watching the world around you crumble, waiting to lose your footing, to drop down into the unknown along with the rest.

Perhaps we've evolved too far. The normality we once found comfort in, the balance we all depended on since life itself was created have been compromised. We've unwillingly traced out our path to destruction . . . You see, I am not mad . . . I merely saw clearly for a second . . . or maybe a minute, or even more than that (I don't quite know for sure for I was not conscious) . . . You see . . . I saw a figure, whose gender I couldn't quite tell, and whose voice I don't recall. It told me this virus was sent down upon the planet as a warning.

Apparently this was the last approach to us humans to make us listen, or rather to feel. To feel the threat, to feel the despair, to feel the need to protect and to be protected, the need to cherish life . . . because at any given moment your right to put your foot outside your house or to breathe clean air without your mouth being covered could be taken from you by force . . . Our instinct for survival was awakened . . . and even that came at a late time, as our planet has been begging for our compassion for a hundred and twenty years. Our Earth needs to breathe clean air again the way we crave to roam around without facial covering. It's been holding its breath for quite a while now and it doesn't want us to suffer the same. (Yes it can get worse than this.)

We witnessed the purity of Earth for a moment with the long quarantine. We saw the pollution rates drop, and the sky clearing up from its toxic greyness, the seas and oceans became almost crystalline again, clear of it's blurry waste. Nature flourished and the natural fragrance of healthy blossoms embraced every particle of oxygen. All this as a consequence of us people stopping for a moment. We stopped and waited, protecting ourselves from this mysterious disease. And the solution to the salvation our home unravelled itself in front of us in the most natural manner.

The veritable remedy to heal our planet is to live with a little more humanity. To use our feet to get to places just like our ancestors did, and to use *public* transport to reach a little further. To consume a little less and reuse a little more. To stop and think about how our daily actions will affect our future. To be more mindful and interested in the smaller problems in order to resolve them and let the bigger ones resolve themselves with time. In any case the big problems we're facing weren't created all at once but grew out of smaller problems, so we need smaller solutions so we can create a bigger one.

I'm sad that we had to be warned by fear . . . Why must humans yield only to terror? Why will they only behave when someone speaks in a sharp and severe tone of voice? Why can't we act through a feeling of love, from the need to preserve our earth so it can keep living along with us — act because life is precious and not because we're afraid of death . . . ?

Now that I've written down the message that was bestowed upon me to deliver, I suppose it could've been an angel that visited me . . . Yes, that would make sense.

April 17th, 2020, CLM (age 15)

"Mortality Support Unit" —
"Temporary mortuary approved for Dorchester"

The new overflow morgue
on the Bridport Road
once housed a radio station.
A famous landmark,
I'd pass it often
on the drive down to see my mother.
The increased deceased
will be accommodated here,
with due compassion and respect.
It will be insulated, boasting bespoke linings,
with an (almost) airtight seal.
Safe, secure, hygienic,
fully temperature-controlled,
chilling down to two degrees —
a large fridge "approved for body storage".
"Worst-case scenario," they say,
"available if required" in May.

Let's hope that there will be
no new *spikes* in demand.

When I went past the spot today
it just gave me the shivers.

April 17th, 2020, JP

THE OLD RADIO STATION

Photos: May 11th, 2020, JP

We are happy to report (May 17th, 2020) that this Mortality Support Facility and another at Poole Port "are standing down owing to a decrease of deaths in the area" (Bournemouth, Christchurch and Poole Council Leader).

A respectful distance

Most parks remain open
but no sitting on the grass,
no sunbathing,
no picnics and no sports.

(You may) walk your dog
(or) exercise.
(You must) stay two metres apart.
(You should) respect others.

Or else the parks will close
as a headless state
struggles to balance
its responsibilities.

April 18th, 2020, AH

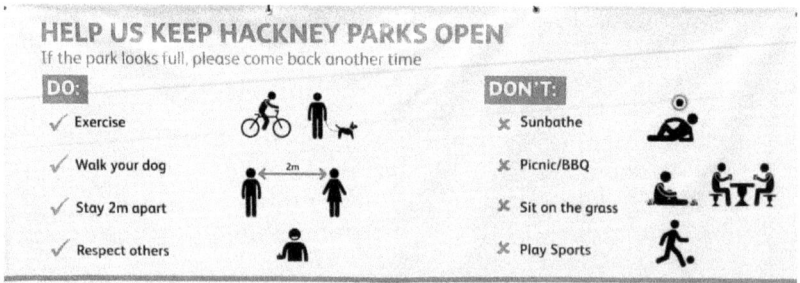

HELP US KEEP HACKNEY PARKS OPEN
If the park looks full, please come back another time

DO:
✓ Exercise
✓ Walk your dog
✓ Stay 2m apart
✓ Respect others

DON'T:
✗ Sunbathe
✗ Picnic/BBQ
✗ Sit on the grass
✗ Play Sports

*Photo: Butterfield Green, London N16, April 18th, 2020, AH
(compare the revised version of the Dos and Don'ts on page 79)*

Socially-distanced birthday quiz

Photo: Brighton, April 19th, 2020, IFR

in a time of coronavirus

she heals
she is my Jesus
she doesn't broadcast it
but she heals

she can fix us
with just a touch
light as a feather leaf
not even as much

the trick is to believe
you can outlast it
that her hands are enough
as they stroke your hair
for the caring love
to overwhelm fear

April 19th/20th, 2020, JN

Apart

Every one of us has a spell
in solitary confinement:
some short, sharp, shedding their souls;
others long, lonely, shredding their hearts.
And twenty-four hours can be a life
that has ears but cannot listen,
has eyes but cannot see,
has hearts but cannot feel.
Oh, how I love the enforced silence
in the sunshine; painting dreams
before I wake from sleeplessness,
alone, friendless and dreamful.
It is my fault for trusting life —
soul mate with only one soul.

Fume your best at what you see
for this is how it will always be;
a love found elsewhere,
in dreams making your daily fare,
sitting by the brook with that vacant stare,
no one caring for you asking if you dare.

There, there, my love, a telephone message
all your hurts and angers did assuage.

April 20th, 2020, FM

Politically speaking

They're "working round the clock"
and "fighting tooth and nail",
they're "straining every sinew"
and "working night and day"
to achieve their target,
now just nine days away:
one hundred thousand tests
per day by the end of April.

Already there's "capacity"
for forty thousand, but
half of that's about the best
    achieved so far . . .

Where can they find more sinews?
How grow more teeth and nails?
How fit more hours round the clock?

The main task now of course —
rig up an explanation,
find a scapegoat, when the last
day of the month arrives.

Failure is not an option —
    politically speaking.

April 21st, 2020, AH
(see also pages 50–52)

A community group notice on the railings of Butterfield Green Playground, London N16
Photo: May 13th, 2020 (AH)

Clap for our heroes

She is a health worker listening out
to millions of hands striking one against the other
every Thursday eve to keep the many
entertained and engaged so the few
can do whatever they deem fit — whatever.

 Clap me no clappings
 Hoop me no hoopings
 Name me no namings
 Grant me no heroics
 Smile me no vacant smilings.

All I ask is for you all
To support an impoverished NHS
To tell our Government to use its hands
To get me personal protection equipment
To recruit trainees with good bursaries.

And to pay me a deserved living wage
To smile when I treat you
Forgive when I keep you waiting
Thank me when I dress your wound
And stand up for me when I am attacked.

 Clap me no clappings
 Hoop me no hoopings
 Name me no namings
 Grant me no heroics
 Grant me not saintliness.

Just treat me as deserved
by paying, protecting, shielding me, and

appreciating that your clappings
fill the air with empty gestures
that help neither me nor my patients.

Thursday, April 23rd, 2020, EE

*A window in Palatine Road, London N16 (Photo: May 20th, 2020, AH).
Poster by Jeremy Deller reproduced with the permission of the house owners and the
publisher of the poster, Fraser Muggeridge Studio. The background consists of four
horizontal bands whose pale colours can't be distinguised in this black-and-white photo.*

Anagram lures OK, Orbis?
or
Taking the P.M. to pieces

BORIS is BIROS,
cheap tools for writing
but nobody writes much today.

And then there's SIR BO —
already benighted,
one day he'll *be* knighted,
perhaps, when it's his time to go.

In India he would be SRI BO
and BORSI in Egypt, of course,
(like a former dictator, you know).

"Going around in circles"
or, more politely, "rotation"
is ORBIS in Latin, *he'll know*
from his posh education.

I ROBS may be
ungrammatical,
but who cares,
if I doesn't get caught.

OBRIS — a Swedish-made sofa
with "inviting proportions"
and very "deep seat" —
clearly just the right sort.

As for BRIÓS
it's Hungarian "brioche",
in case you want
something to eat.

With an extra O
off he can go
to sunny I-ta-lee
where BRIOSO is "lively"
and SOBRIO's "sober",
but I don't think
that can be he,

for SOBRÌ means he "sips"
and SOBRI means "Sip!"
and I don't think that'll be tea.

Add a touch of garlic
and "Boris" becomes
BORSAIOLO —
a cutpurse, you see.

Written April 2nd, 2020, withheld until
April 28th (see page 23), AH

(position of stress on the Italian words:
bri-*o*-so | *so*-bri-o | so-*brì* | *so*-bri | bor-sai-*o*-lo)

47

Another Slough

Come friendly virus, instruct Trump.
He's turned his country to a dump,
For hate-filled lies in ears to pump.
Swarm over, Death!

Come Covid, blow to smithereens
Those re-election plans he schemes,
Tinned fake, tinned misanthrope, tinned dreams,
Tinned minds, tinned breath.

Mess up the mess they call the clown
A president who should go down
As one-term wearer of the crown
Please, no more years.

And get that man with double chin
Who'll always cheat and always win,
Who washes his repulsive skin
In women's tears:

And smash his desk of polished oak
And smash his hands so used to stroke
And stop his boring dirty joke
And make him yell.

But spare the foolish folk who add
Credence to the stinking cad;
It's not their fault that they are mad,
They've tasted Hell.

It's not their fault they do not know
It's bullshit on the radio,
It's not their fault he is their foe
They are misled

And talk of support from TV star
With various bogus cures to mar
He dares to blame some from afar.
It's on his head.

Keeping aloof at home, with care
His quiff of fake peroxide hair
He dries it in his fetid air
And Leading — fails.

Come friendly virus and dry cough
Warn him that he may shuffle off
For Covid cares not for the toff;
The earth exhales.

April 29th, 2020, BJ

*With gratitude to the late John Betjeman for his poem
"Slough", which provided the model, and from which
stanzas 4 and 5 have been taken over unchanged.*

A triumph for the minister
on May Day

So, must I eat my words?
They did it. They achieved
their goal, politically speaking:
A hundred thousand tests
on April thirtieth.

There had been modest increases
but on the twenty-ninth
the goal was still far off.
A monumental fudge
was what they needed now —

a Herculean Labour
by Labour Day or else
failure and ridicule would follow.
But they'd been labouring "tirelessly"
(vehicles without tyres come to mind)
and the Wheels of State were turning.

Already they'd a system
of online application:
testing for all deemed
"eligible". The system crashed
by ten o'clock the first two days.

Many, it's true, got their appointments,
not always in the right place, though.
Some southerners were offered tests
in Scotland, for example.

The real stroke of genius, came

with the home-testing kits,
and almost forty thousand
of these were posted off
on April thirtieth.

No matter that the post
is slow and unreliable
these days. Within a week or so
many of the forty thousand tests
for April thirtieth will have
been done, the goal achieved,
rash promises fulfilled —
politically speaking;
but ridicule can hardly be avoided.

It was "a national achievement"
according to the minister.
Was there a typo or did he just
misread the script? It was indeed
a *notional* achievement.
That we can all agree.

Not only have they now achieved
a hundred thousand tests a day —
by sleight of hand and on
a single day — but far exceeded it
by twenty-two-point-three-four-seven percent
(by sleight of hand and on a single day).

But now at least we know —
test or no test — we're all
zinc-plated, if that helps:
"Setting stretching ambitious
goals in a national crisis

has a galvanising effect
on everyone involved."

"That it was an audacious goal,"
the minister knew well. "We needed
an audacious goal," he said.
But even more *audacious* now
the May Day self-congratulation.
All the bereaved, the dead, the suffering,
the dying, and the nurses, doctors,
NHS porters, drivers, cleaners,
the local volunteers, the carers
deserve far better than the brash
dishonesty of this, his May-Day triumph.

The HSJ (Health Service Journal)
has claimed that until recently
tests were included in the daily
count only *after* they'd been sent
to a laboratory. The government
denies there's been a change
in the way the numbers are collated.
The HSJ insists there *has* been,
and all because the minister's
"obsessed" with honouring his pledge.
(If only honour'd played a part in this!)

But who's been *tested* by the pledge?
Remember Belshazzar's feast?
 "The writing on the wall"?

WEIGHED IN THE BALANCE AND FOUND WANTING

May 2nd, 2020, AH
(see also page 42)

CT Scanners

My brother and I
inside separate CT scanners,
by chance the self-same day,
the twenty-third of April —
his in Somerset, mine in Dorset.
They scan our limbs and organs.
We hide our fears of nosocomial infection.
I have to wait in untied gown,
claustrophobic inside my cubicle,
for an emergency Covid patient
who's wheeled in — he's near death's door.
I hear everything that's said.
They clean the surfaces well, I'm told.
As I breathe in and hold my breath,
I wonder how many hours,
the virus survives in air.
Up to three hours, the scientists state.

Breathe out! — the disembodied voice.
Four more days until I know . . .
For my brother,
four more months of pain.

May 3rd, 2020, JP
(see also page 14)

May 2020

Trump is saying that sixty thousand plus dead
Is quite acceptable when the economy needs opening
Even up to one hundred thousand, or thereabouts as long
As he can start campaigning in rallies.
The desire for re-election surmounts any care
For the little man in the street, struggling to pay
This month's rent and feed the family on $1200 — the stimulus
Cheque sent to cover your bills for at least three months!

Cry freedom, cry freedom and let's keep our guns
End this lockdown, this "shelter in place"
I've a right to be dying if that's what I choose; I don't care
About you or your elderly parent, or the kid who is sick, or your
Not-yet-buried. My rights trump yours any time of the day.

So what, that New York has so many dead, so what
That the sick keep on coming; so what that you can't afford care.
Do you think that your worries are my concern? Think again,
    little man
Because Melania's "I really don't care, do you?" is my go-to
    mantra
In these trying times.

Liberate Michigan, liberate Minnesota, while we're at it, let's
    liberate Virginia too
Those damned democrats trying to save your lives with their
    lockdowns and advice
For staying alive. Y'all need to start protests, and carry your guns,
and don't wear that face mask, forget social distancing, go out
and hug, get real close to those strangers in crowds
Cos nothing shouts freedom quite like catching the virus and
    dying today.

May 3rd, 2020, SW

54

Inaction and reaction
are unequal and apposite

Now that their slowness to take action
way-back in March is under scrutiny,
they still insist that all along they "made
the right decisions at the right time"
and "on the basis of medical advice".
(Good Doctor Cummings comes to mind,
his active participation in SAGE
meetings not at that time disclosed.)

There is no question, it just isn't possible
that government inaction
(on medical advice) could be
in any way responsible
for deaths (potentially some thousands)
that might otherwise have not occurred,
for "right decisions" simply can't be wrong.

It's simply inconceivable —
the medicine cabinet can't possibly
be charged with peddling the wrong remedy!
That's the bottom line I fear.
(You couldn't get much lower.)

May 4th, 2020, AH

SAGE is the UK government's Scientific
Advisory Group for Emergencies.

Isolated

Self-portrait, iPad painting, May 4th, 2020, SFR

Lockdown on a summer's day

Cruellest April makes way for marvellous May
mixing the memory, distorting the desire.
For God has played his hand,
shuffling a shipwreck of confusion
with a sardonic smile:
Lockdown meets longing.

In the woods outside, the bluebells
have bled their joy. And now the buttercups
wave a yellow flag
to signal there's disease on board.

Meantime, inside the sterile house
the President purrs his ironic lines
Just You, Just Me as the saxophone
scratches a comma in a sentence without clarity.

T. S. Eliot and Lester Young make
a heady concoction, a disparate wasteland
of connection in the storm.
And I say to God: you discharge your anger
with a mischievous twist.
What now? And for your next trick?

May 5th, 2020, MA

Clumsy haiku

How many Oxford PPEs
does it take
to get some PPE?

May 5th, 2020, IW

Covid-Nineteen War Cabinet
reconsidered

The virus cannot be our "enemy",
for it's devoid of all intention
and harbours no hostility
nor any other feeling. Blindly
it seeks the openings our way
of life abundantly provides
for it to propagate itself.
It's just a force of nature — what
insurers call an "Act of God".
We're being killed by accident
as far as it's concerned.

We might say, though,
that it's a warning shot
fired across our bows
from some future sea
which we
may not be sailing.

May 6th, 2020, AH
(see also page 24)

Dorset Blues

They've caught the fish.
They've shorn the sheep.
No exports now.
The shepherds weep.

May 6th, 2020, JP

#clapforourcarers haiku

Thursdays 8 p.m.
we're all outdoors and standing
in our front gardens.

        My wife beats a drum
        (pan, with wooden spoon), I clap
        till my hands are red.

Among our neighbours
two have small brass bells to shake
one blows a trumpet.

        From across the street
        people that we scarcely know
        wave to us and smile.

When this is over
will life return to normal?
Well, let's hope not quite.

Thursday, May 7th, 2020, AH

In colour
on the
back
cover

It's not a monster

Painting: May 7th, 2020, OW, age 7

Phone conversation
AH: Your mum sent me your picture of a monster.
OW: It's not a monster. I was just doodling.
AH: OK, but I really like it. I'd like to put it in the book.
OW: It's got nothing to do with Covid.

But it is a nice example of creative things families have been doing in Lockdown. In this case making their own pigments for their paintings.

Home Studio

We ground up red and grey brick with stones, and boiled up beetroot. We then made egg tempera using egg-yolk, as per the old masters.

May 17th, 2020, PH

Photos: May 7th, 2020, PH

Dodona Oracle

The leaves are not rustling,
the pigeons don't fly —
wild flowers are saying
"You'll live till you die."

Undated, JP

Trees in recovery

The "essential work" of repaving the pavements
in our street started weeks before the Lockdown;
stalled for a while; and then resumed, but with
a smaller gang of the contractor's men.

The work proceeded much more slowly, but,
almost completed now, it's very good
to see replacing trees — which in the course
of many years had died or lost their arguments
with vehicles — considered to be part
of that "essential work".

           And nine or ten
young saplings, of various size and species,
now fill the gaps, though some look a bit floppy
still, struggling to recover from their transplants.

May 8th, 2020, AH

Passing

The starched white pillow
crisp as frost
cupped my head softly.

To my right my long time
fellow traveller
who had passed recently
held out his hand
like Michelangelo's David
beckoning me to come
welcoming me home.

To my left my dear children,
hunched and short of breath
yearned for me to stay,
to defy death, and wept.

The window in my room
glowed white through the glass
and bathed me in light
as I closed my eyes and slept.
I went without a secret kept.

May 8th, 2020, JN

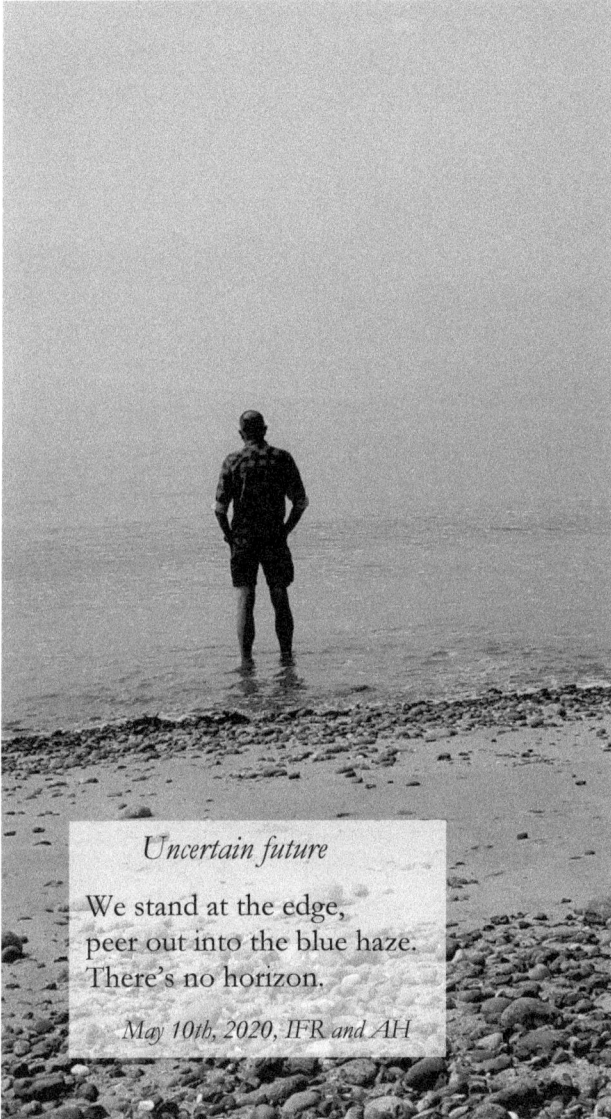

Uncertain future

We stand at the edge,
peer out into the blue haze.
There's no horizon.

May 10th, 2020, IFR and AH

Photo: May 8th, 2020, IFR

Boris has spoken . . .

Morn-ing has bro - ken like the first morn - ing, black - bird has spo - ken like the first bird.

Opening words of the hymn by Eleanor Farjeon with its traditional Scottish tune.

Last night on television the P.M.
addressed the nation — almost half of it
(watched, it is said, by twenty-seven million),
leaving "Britain divided and confused",
as *The Guardian* headline pronounced today.

His appearance on our screens
    (someone had combed his hair),
his sober demeanour, and his smooth
    and (for once) well-rehearsed
delivery of a (for once) well-crafted
    (by someone) speech —
well-crafted, I mean, linguistically,
    and not in its chaotic messages —
gave me the first inkling that this man
    might have become a statesman
and not just the buffoon who ever since
his stint as Foreign Secretary to May
has been a national embarrassment,
if, that is, he'd set his sights on something
    other than his personal power.

64

His grip on power, though, has not
been equal to the challenge of a virus.
The other "nations" of the "Union"
refuse to follow where he leads
and he's "BECOME," as Ian Blackford,
Member for Ross, Skye and Lochaber
and leader of the SNP at Westminster,
informed him on video in the Commons,
"THE PRIME MINISTER OF ENGLAND."

May 11th, 2020, AH

(On May10th Boris Johnson had
announced "plans" for the easing of Lockdown.)

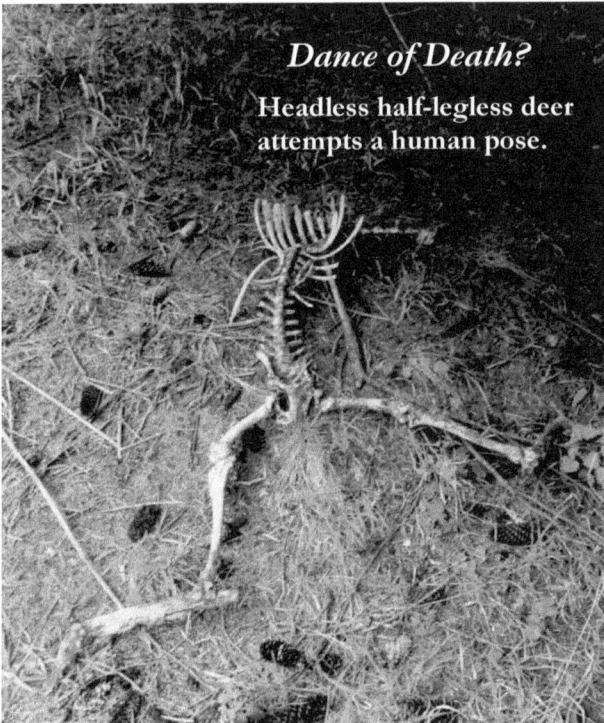

Words and photo (in woodland near Ludlow), AH

65

Conscious isolation

The thing with isolation is that it's really very isolating
It drives you somewhat crazy if you are that way inclined
You walk around confused and start to talk out loud
You treat yourself as listener and speaker and even argue
      back
The point you just so carefully made with arguments
      more brilliant
Than you've ever used before:

The world is round, we know it is because you can't fall
      off a non-existent edge
And anyway, the astronauts took pictures showing a
      circle of blue and green,
It must be said that flat earth believers are a somewhat
      strangely bunch!
No, no, you cry to you alone; it must be flat because I
      can see for miles
And there is an edge which you are calling an horizon.
Our ancestors had it right; flat is flat and how account
      for those who sailed off merrily
And never ever came back home?

Let's call a truce on that one then and argue something
      different, like is the air really there?
Of course it is, you breathe it every day. Why doesn't it
      run out when there are so many here?
Because, you fool; who are you calling a fool? I know I'm
      always right and this argument is just silly now. We
      both agree that we are here in solitary solidarity
So let's shake hands and have a cup of tea.

I'm going out for my daily exercise to walk around the block;
     but I don't want to go just yet
Your other side declares. Oh not again, why must you always
     disagree with me?
We're on the same side here you know; we must keep fit and
     eat our greens
And walk or run around — before I go though here's a
     question for you:
Does my backside look big in these new leggings? If I say
     yes I'll never hear the last of it
And if I say no I'll know I'm lying to myself. I think it's time
     for chocolate in every shape and form so let's go and
     sit and chomp away because there's ages to the
     summer and we don't care if that bikini doesn't fit!

May 13th, 2020, SW

Unconscious isolation

The Queen Mother in splendid unconscious isolation in the fog. Queen Mother Square, Poundbury, Dorchester. (Photo: JP)

Who's for shearing?

Blah Blah, Baksheesh,
where's that P.P.E.?
All going back to Turkey?
Dearie, dearie me.

Such mismanagement
and who can be to blame?
The strategists in government
should hang their heads in shame.

Blah Blah, Baksheesh . . .
Lifting Lockdown? Load of bull.
Covid's still around
and now the parks are full.

A cough for the Master,
a coffin for the Dame,
one parent for the little boy
who lives down the lane.

May 13th, 2020, DJ

Bumble Boy Blue

Bumble Boy blue,
    Covid-planning forlorn,
Mustique's in his diary,
    a new baby's born.

Where is the man
    with a promise to keep?
He's under his hairstack,
    fast asleep.

Will you not wake him?
    Oh no not I,
for if I do,
    he's sure to lie!

May 14th, 2020, BJ

I Miss You Guys

I wish I was back at school.
Instead, at home while I weep and bawl,
I miss my friends I wish this would end,
I feel like everything will descend.

But look, a light in the distance,
but everyone walks by like it has no existence,
I follow that light the last bit of hope.

Suddenly I fall down a mystical slope,
into a land where the corona is gone,
but no one is drawn to their devices,
it's like everyone's heart rises,
everyone is talking,
and all are walking,
not using silly machines like cars
(they should be put behind bars).

And then I see
the older me,
playing with my friends.
They all have different minds,
not talking about games and phones,
playing together instead of alone.

Look, the light is back,
A thing has changed and my heart has no crack,
because I know there is hope.
Yes there is hope,
there is hope,
there is HOPE.
Yes there is hope,

so next time you're down,
do not frown,
there is

HOPE

May 14th, 2020, WM (age 10)

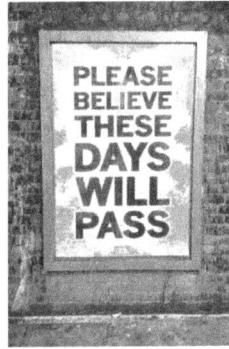

Photo: Green Lanes, London N4,
April 30th, 2020, PH

This poem and "Life" by Albie Waddell on page 72 were
written as part of an online poetry project during Lockdown,
set by their class teacher Ella Martin. These were the
instructions: "The title of your poem is 'A day in the life' and
it's all about you. More specifically, it's about how your life
has changed since school closed and the Lockdown began."

Convalescent

A chaffinch singing,
here beside the River Frome.
I'm convalescing.

May 15th, 2020, JP

Life

There are up-and-downs in life
And Covid is an example of strife
But we must try not to be down
And we will survive this Lockdown

I work on the computer every day
Even if it is sunny outside in May
Not by choice, but I must learn
To keep my mind off this horrible germ

I can't see my family or friends
If I could, I think that would make amends
To all the sorrow in our hearts
And hopefully Covid won't go right off the charts

To use up your time you can bake cakes
Even if you end up with a load of mistakes
I wish for so much more
Like, to be with you throughout this war
I miss you all

May 15th, 2020, AW (age 10)

(see the note on page 71)

The XMASk

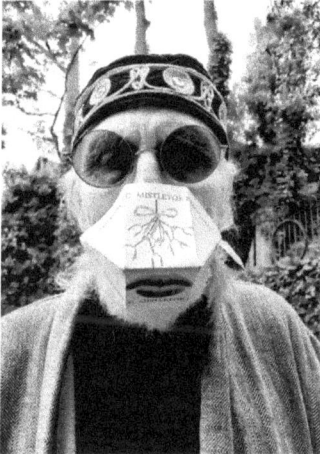

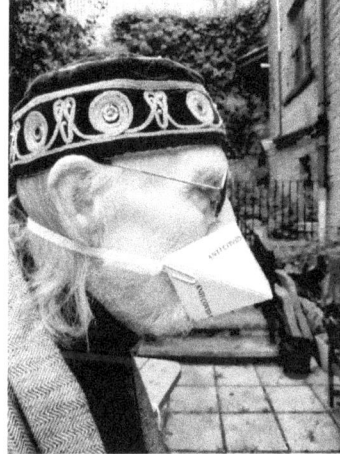

On the left, Wilf Lunn models his original Anti Swine Flu Mistletoe Kissing Mask, produced in 2009 when the French government banned kissing in schools. On the right he gives us a side view of the new and redesigned Anti Covid-19 version of the Anti-Kissing (or Aunty-Kissing) Mask, also known, since it's for the festive kissing season, as the XMASk.

Photos: May 15th, 2020, DJ. Text: WL, DJ, AH.

Below is a reduced-size black-and-white image of the new XMASk. A colour image can be seen on the back cover.

ANTI COVID-19 MISTLETOE KISSING MASK

fold inwards

fold inwards

ANTI COVID-19 MISTLETOE KISSING MASK

Cruise ships in Weymouth Bay

Cruise ships — Marella, Cunard, P&O —
laid-up liners securely anchored
off Weymouth's shore
strung out in a line, bridging the bay,
avoiding all the mooring fees.

These luxury floating hotels — we locals
like to gaze at them — rusting resorts
where everything on board's in mothballs.

But floating prisons for their crews —
engineers, officers (well-paid, well-fed)
and low-paid deckhands far from home.
All taking their daily Covid tests.
Some in quarantine, confined to quarters.

Others seen ashore in Weymouth,
or Portland, huddled in groups, lost souls
loitering around the dismal docks,
not made welcome in Weymouth's bars.

Cruise ships riding at anchor, turning slowly,
moving with the wind and tides.
Ghosts ships with their skeleton crews.

May 16th, 2020, JP

Staff Conference by Zoom

We should have been flying to Paris —
another meeting where ambitions are killed.

More targets and "strategic plans" —
the uncertain thoughts of also-rans.

Tinker here and tinker there,
give the staff a nasty scare.

Mute me now, I can't pretend —
no-one knows where this will end.

Rearrange the jars, my friends,
We know you know the cupboard's bare.

May 16th, 2020, JP

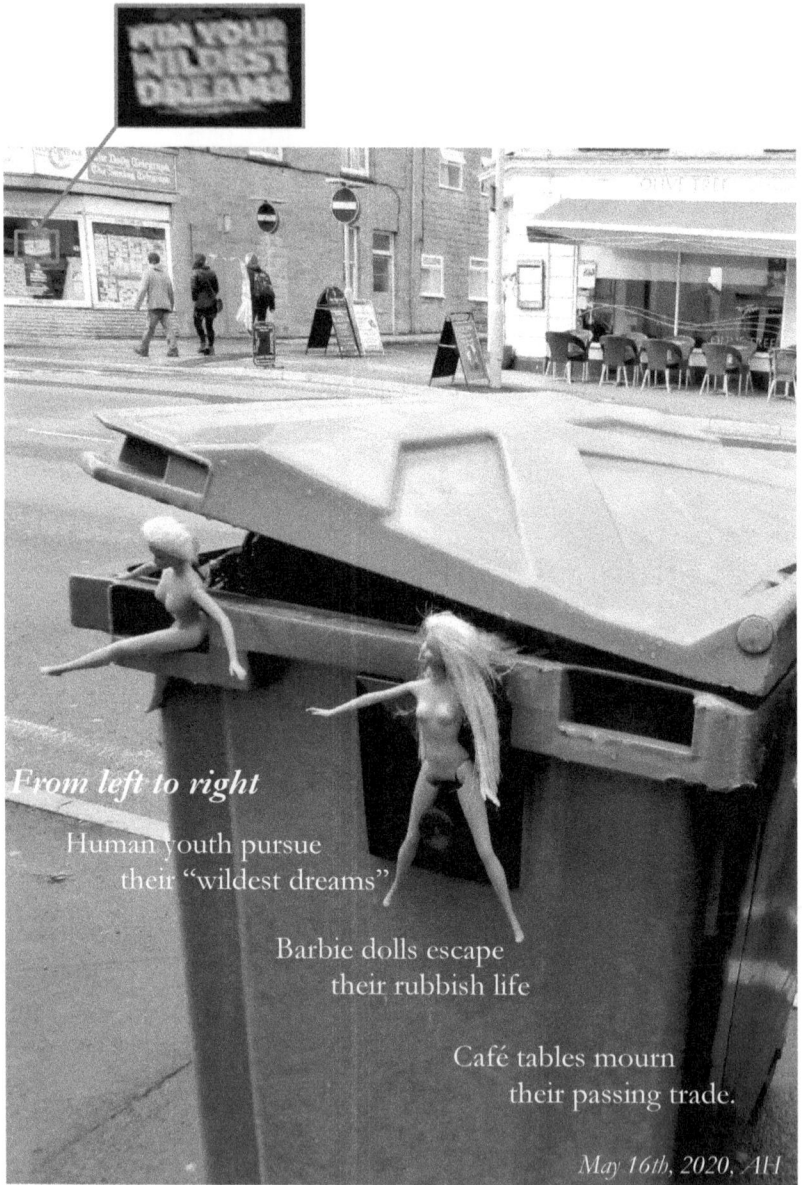

From left to right

Human youth pursue
their "wildest dreams"

Barbie dolls escape
their rubbish life

Café tables mourn
their passing trade.

May 16th, 2020, AH

Photo: Bridport, Spring, JP

Song without words
or
Praise for the handling of the crisis
by UK and US governments

At any time from February to May 17th, 2020 and beyond, Anon.

Sounds of Lockdown

Waking up to no sounds
        no alarm no cars
              and no footsteps
                        on the pavement
                              under the window
The insistent quiet
        inside and outside

Wind in the trees
        in the garden
                humming insects and birds
                        lots of birds
Ambulance sirens wailing
                down the hill
                        from the hospital
The slow pit-pat
        of bored one-player swing-ball
                        next door
The frequent pinging
                of new group messages
                        and emails
Skylarks singing along
            to walks
                over green hills
The clapping
        and the clanging
                of pots and pans
                        on Thursday evenings
Every night
        the midnight rumble
                        of a skateboard passing by

And every day
        punctuated
                by Trumpet Boy's
                        four-thirty p.m.
                                street serenade

May 17th, 2020, IFR

Out of the woods?

Photo: near Much Hadham, Hertfordshire, May 19th, 2020, AH

Help us keep Hackney safe for everyone
If the park looks full, please come back another time or go to another park

DO:
✓ Stay local
✓ **Keep 2 metres apart** from those not in your household
✓ Take rubbish home
✓ Enjoy the park and respect others

The signs they are a changin'

DON'T:
✗ Gather in groups of more than two people from different households
✗ BBQ
✗ Play group sports
✗ Use closed facilities

Photo: Butterfield Green, London N16, May 20th, 2020, AH
(compare the earlier version of the Dos and Don'ts on page 38)

(THIS WAS THE FINAL PAGE OF *VIRAL VERSE*)

Lockdown Lament

I miss the little things in life:
the going out, the coming back,
the noise of children off to school
forgetting others don't have to be up.
The quiet streets, the empty playground —
until four o'clock when the young come home.

I hear the birds tweeting to their chicks,
rustle of leaves around the nest,
the chirrup of gaping mouths
reminds us of the life which grows
resisting pain and deadly disease
in clean fresh air from lack of cars.

I see the leaves on endless trees and
the blooms of early flowers bright
in reds, yellows, blues and white, their
heads nodding at the sun and smiling bright as
the grass grows long; the daisies rise
and bumble bees project their hum.

It seems the little things in life
turn out to be the biggest joys
in days that pass in peaceful ways.
And soon enough the times will change
with busyness returning, whilst memories
of these quiet hours tug quietly at our thoughts.

May 24th, 2020, SW

Let's tell sad stories

He sat straight most royally
in the Rose Garden spring sun.
Millions stared, ears bent, keen to listen.
"For God's sake, let us sit upon the ground
And tell sad stories of exigent circumstance.
How the virus struck,
haunting our days and deposing our peace.
How childcare dictated
journeys so long and farewells to home
eye sight impaired, tested aright by a short drive.
I understand your anger,
yet *you have but mistook me all this while:*
I live with bread like you, feel want,
Taste grief, need friends.
I did what any father would,
behaved as every husband should.
Rien de rien. Non, je ne regrette rien.
Now I will take questions,
one from each of you.
We're all in this together.
Laura, fire away, you go first."
And there stood a rose amongst roses
and spoke French as every great one does:
"Tu le connais, lecteur, ce monstre délicat,
Hypocrite lecteur, — mon semblable, — mon frère!"

May 26th, 2020, FM

Quotations (in italics): the first two from Shakespeare's *Richard II*, Act III, scene ii; the third from Edith Piaf's memorable song: "Nothing at all. No, I regret nothing"; and the last from Baudelaire's "Au lecteur" in *Les fleurs du mal*: "You know him, reader, this exquisite monster, / Hypocrite reader, my double, my brother!".

STOP PRESS
NEW EYE-TESTING PROCEDURES

**THE GOVERNMENT OF
ENGLAND, WONDERLAND AND NARNIA
has issued the following new guidelines to opticians
for effective eye testing.**

1. Eye tests may only be carried out when bluebells are in flower (usually late April–May). For exemptions, please advise patients to download and fill in the appropriate form, available here:

www.eyes.gov.ewn/bb-woods-4joe_public

2. Prior to the test, patients will need to obtain a car and a four-year-old child (wife optional; no husbands, please, unless certified fit for childcare). In exceptional circumstances, teenage female relations may be used in place of a wife.

3. Patients are requested, but not obliged, to supply up-to-date certificates of lie-detector testing. The government is currently on-target to carry out 100,000 of these tests every five minutes. Senior government officials are permitted (indeed, encouraged) to supply redacted test results.

4. In order to ensure adequate protection for the optician administering the test, all contact with the patient is to be via video link and e-mail. Psychological support and post-traumatic-eye-test counselling is also available to participating opticians.

5. In order to ensure the safety of all children involved in testing procedures, strict child protection measures are in place (but do not apply to the children of senior government officials, who are advised to use their instincts).

6. The test is to be self-administered by the patient, and recorded in the form of a vlog, which should then be sent to the optician's e-mail account. Senior government officials are advised to supply appropriately edited videos.

7. The test consists of driving thirty miles down the road, with a 4-year-old child (and, if so-desired, a wife, certified child-care-competent husband or teenage female relation). The destination is to be a bluebell wood, so patients will need to plan their route very carefully, if necessary driving a few hundred miles to an appropriate location in advance.

8. The test should be recorded on a dashboard camera or, preferably, a hand-held mobile device. The patient is required to speak while driving and filming, to give the optician a clear picture of his competence to drive (and ability to see while so doing). The optician should be alert to any signs of visual impairment on the part of the driver, but should not hesitate to rely primarily on the driver's own assessment.

9. This test is only available to men at present. Written permission should be sought in advance from the mothers of the 4-year-old children involved. Mothers should be warned that failure to co-operate may result in fines and, in extreme cases, imprisonment.

May 26th, 2020, SE

Home Schooling — A Modern Qasidah

"BACK to school today.
bank holiday weekend
Today, we home school,
my pupils keen to learn.

You two have had your way,
shrieking, guffawing and crying.
the teacher, I, and you,
Here goes, children. Silence!"

"DO WE have to mum?
homework is my ENEMY.
"Don't start 'No! No! No!'
she's almost finished her sums

I hate maths and
Shan't do it. Shan't. Shan't."
Look at your sister
while you make silly faces."

HE SHRIEKS. He weeps.
feels sick and, even,
"Okay! Don't learn
and grow like uncle Tommy

He loses his pen and
pukes his breakfast on his sums.
and be a stupid boy
and go to prison too . . ."

SILENCE. The odd sob
punctuated by a girl's voice:

and some lingering sighs
"Finished mummy. Can I do
                more sums?"

Loud whisperings float away:
Another shriek and sobbing

"Swat. Boffin. Creep."
and sound of footsteps receding.

"RIGHT! No elevenses for you.
every sum on that page.

You will sit there till you do
Come Louise, we'll have milk and
                biscuits."

Interregnum. Loud sighs.
Papers rustling. Pen scratching.

Occasional animal shrieks.
Clap. Shout of delight.

"FINISHED mum. All sums
                done."
But, son, they are all wrong."

"Oh, good boy. Here's a biscuit
                for you too.
"Mu'umm! You just said, to finish
                them . . ."

May 27th, 2020, EE

Pontius the Pilot
and the Flight into Edict

The Moving Tweeter Tweets; and, having Twit,
Moves on: nor all thy Piety nor Wit
Shall lure it back to cancel half a Line,
Nor all thy Snears cross out a Word of it.
Repinned from
The Ruby Hat of O Ma, Come On

The Mighty Tweeter wants to shut down Twitter
for violating Freedom of Expression.
His Freedom. His Expression. Total Freedom
to propagate whatever Words of Wisdom
His Great Bird Brain concocts and beak puts forth,
without the fear of being contradicted,
fact-checked or subject to the slightest scrutiny.

The Avian Good Genius never errs.
"Let there be Light," He says, and Light there is.
The Universe is subject to His Laws.

No irony can penetrate His Hide.
He thinks Tweet Masters have indulged in censorship.
Great Bird Brain cannot grasp it's He Who wants
to censor *everyone* who dares to gainsay Him.

WHAT I HAVE WRITTEN I HAVE WRITTEN
the One Great Pilate in the Sky declaims.

May 29th, 2020, AH

The background to the title is a Sunday School anecdote. A child, having
listened to various Bible stories, draws a picture of a plane with one man
in the cockpit and in the back a man and woman in robes, the woman
holding a baby. Asked to explain, the child points to the man in the
cockpit, "That's Pontius the pilot on the flight into Egypt."

Loot'n' shoot'n' gun-toot'n' Presidump
or
Twitter Moderators take on Trump

In Minneapolis we all have seen
on our TVs or phones a white police officer,
while making an arrest, kneeling
for several minutes on a black man's neck.
The result a *cardiac* arrest.

The most we're told George Floyd had done was try
to spend a phoney twenty-dollar bill.
If twenty dollars is the price of life
how far, then, was this US citizen
from Slavery? Do BLACK LIVES really MATTER,
Officer? *Do* they, Mister President?

The people of the city, whites among the blacks,
take to the streets in anger, overflowing
into violence against property.
Police precinct broken into, set on fire.

Trump takes to Twitter to announce
that "When the looting starts, the shooting starts".
The Moderators act. The Tweet's obscured.
 "By glorifying violence," they explain,
it breaks their rules. But for a man empowered
to give the order for the shooting,
it's rather more than that — a threat to kill.
It authorizes non-judicial executions,
capital punishment for theft and arson.

It's hard to think
how much further down than this

a man entrusted with so much
responsibility could sink.
He's placed himself *beneath* contempt —
some *twenty thousand leagues beneath* . . .

So I here I stop — there's nothing more to say
— today . . .
                    But, No, we can't let this day close
without a note on two more policy
announcements that he made today
(both part of brinkmanship with China):
he'll finally cut US funds
to WHO and terminate
the special trading status of Hong Kong.

Hard *not* to think of "baby", "toys",
      and "throwing out" and "pram".
          If he keeps up this pace
                then nuclear war
                may be no more
                    than days
                    away!

May 29th, 2020, AH

Postscript to the above

Speaking of nuclear war, just two days later,
the evening of the thirty-first of May,
Trump was conducted to the White House Bunker
to shield him from protesters at the gates.

June 1st, 2020, AH

Comorbidity and Charon

Yes, I may be more vulnerable than some,
at higher risk than others.
I'm older now than many
in the general population.
I have underlying conditions:
I'm susceptible to heartbreak,
to loneliness and stress,
to the urge to see a secret lover,
at my second home in France.
I'll take a chance, my only chance
to make my way to Arcachon.
My co-driver might be — take a guess! —
a furloughed ferryman and psychopomp —
we're on good terms, I know him well,
he's up to date with shifting freight,
he'll find a way to sneak my car on.

May 29th, 2020, JP

two- and three-season tanka

This amazing spring
everything in the garden
seems to bloom at once
but by the height of summer
the colours may have faded.

In this our Plague Spring
the falling leaves of autumn
are too far off to see
and winter still lies buried
under a blanket of fear.

May 31st, 2020, AH

Age of Innocence
(England in the '60s)

Remember the Corona man?
who came in his Corona van
deliv'ring fizzy drinks and not
the kiss of death.

May 31st, 2020, AH

(Photo by kind permission of The Stilltime Collection)

The perils of graphic design

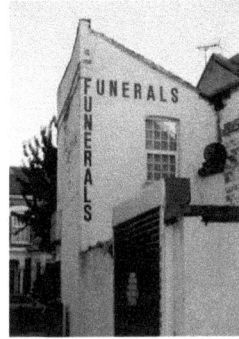

What you write
may not always
be read
the way
that you want it
to be
and for
an undertaker
one might say
CARELESS WORDS COST DEATHS
especially in an age of misinformation
on a presidential scale,
selective quotation, fake news,
every customer a smart phone
in their hand and so much
potential business to be lost.

Text: June 1st, 2020, AH

*Photo: Kersley Road,
London N16,
May 31st, 2020, AH*

Boris addresses the nation

Now look here, um, you, er, plebs and gentlemen, and um, respected — if you know what I mean — members of the electorate, as it were, vox populi vox dei, OK? Or, to put it in the vernacular, the, er, people have, um, spoken and their Brexit god is Boris, that's, er, in fact, me. So what we're, er, er, calling on you to, um, do today, and not just, er, today, but, um, in the Cummings days, civic duty and all that, er, civile, si ergo, fortibus es in ero, as the man said, and what the eye doesn't see — I mean, look, you've got to, we've all got to, have to, er, be a bit sensible about this, use your, er, instincts, OK, and it's one rule for you as is only, um, right and, er, proper. Homo sum, iacta alea est, nil nisi bonum, nil by mouth and, er, er, kindly put a sock in it. Thank you. In fact, actually, er, look at it another, um, way, I am actually going to take forty buses and er, put them in a, as it were, row, and yes, going to, er, have words on the, um, if you can picture this, um, sides. Thought about my old school er, motto, can't — if only could — quite call to mind, er, er, remember what was, but Latin anyway, and none of your pig's or pope's Latin (no disrespect to, er, the holy fathers, farm animals, what that might be, er, said to be) but the real McCoy there. But Dom, you know, right-hand man, er, good chap, wrong school, poor bugger, but can't be helped — no mottoes there, mens sana in corpore sano; not even rugger for the buggers, um, but as I say, if you, er, know what I mean, anyway, old Dom, fully compos mentis — good eyesight, too — ne plus ultra — mirabile visu — he wasn't really on the buses thing himself. Said it could, um, possibly, er, be thought, well by some, to, er, equate to a pons asinorum in er, some, er, respects. Not disrespects, though, as we, er, agreed. But anyway, er, carry on regardless, up the er, er, buses, as I quipped, and well, poor old Dom, still a bit tired after all that, er, driving, so got on and did it my, er, self, no point hanging about. Right? So, what you er, plebs, and er, gentleman and, um vectors, and, er, symptom-free offspring back at school must, and I er, er, repeat, must NOT forget is that it is, always has been and shall remain the fact that, er, and not forgetting, um, civic, er, duty, dulce et decorum est pro patria mori, coming soon to a, um, bus near you. Thank you very much.

June 1st, 2020, SE

Remember Boris's Lies-and-Broken-Promises Big Bed Brexit Buses in 2016? (AH)

No safe place for angels
(Abney Park Cemetery, London N16)

Dotted here and there
    along the curving avenues,
In among the tumbled
    or still tumbling older
Monuments, some War Graves
    Commission headstones:
Upright, small, white, uniform,
    and free of undergrowth.

Many of the angels too
    might be considered
Casualties, or Mutilés
    de Guerre, for more than
Half of them have lost
    one hand or arm,
Sev'ral have lost both, and
    some are even headless.

Winged or wingless, let us say
    that all are angels,
Or else angels in the making —
    forms of those who've died.
Not yet any Fallen
    Angels I can see.
Some will fall, there is no doubt,
    before too long.

Some of them play safe and keep their hands
Close to their bodies or else they clutch a cross.

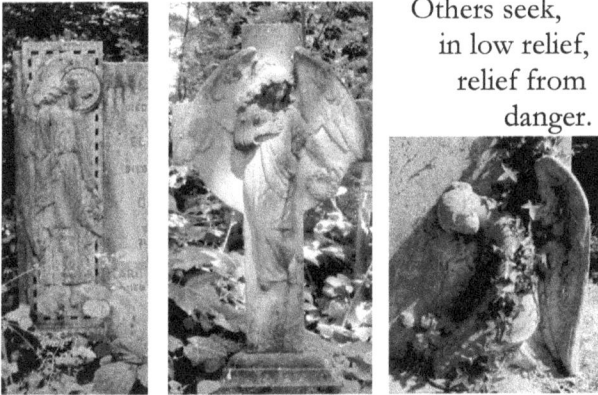

Others seek,
in low relief,
relief from
danger.

Where are all their missing hands today?
This intimidating obelisk accounts for only one.
Are the rest all gone? or lost in undergrowth?
Pocketed perhaps by curio hunters, sold at
Boot sales, proudly placed on mantelshelves
In carefully restored Victorian homes?

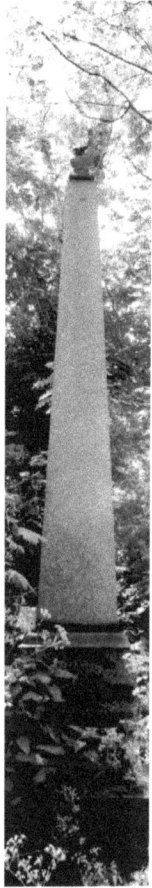

There are recent burials too
    in Abney Park,
Some very recent.
    Date of "Sunset"
For this nonagenarian —
    MUM, NAN, SIS
Spelled out in flowers —
    is given as the fifth of April,
Twenty-twenty. And a loose
    memorial stone
Hand-painted, no larger
    than a smallish loaf,
Laid among some small loose rocks —
    there is no-body here —

tells us of a death the twelfth
    or thirteenth day of May.
AND SO
PERHAPS
IT IS
THAT HERE
WE READ
THE NAMES
OF
TWO MORE
VICTIMS
OF
THE
VIRUS

June 2nd, 2020, AH
Photos: May 30th & June 2nd, 2020, AH

We're in Big Trouble

"If I'm the smartest guy in the room,
we're in big trouble" says Max Brooks — his novel
World War Z predicted the pandemic —
being modest, interviewed by Hadley Freeman,
Guardian Review, Saturday the 6th of June.

Let's get a load of T-shirts printed quick — freebies
for all the UK Cabinet and White House Staff,
including those two self-styled geniuses in charge.

To inculcate a little modesty — if that is possible.

June 7th, 2020, AH

IF **I'M** THE
SMARTEST GUY
IN THE ROOM
**WE'RE IN
BIG
TROUBLE**

Design: AH

Meditation on two added words

Photo: Butterfield Green, London N16, June 8th, AH

Whether just by accident
or selected with great care
the red marker that was used
for the two words added to
this plastic banner matches
perfectly the colour of
the red parts of the printing.

I would so much like to know
what was going on inside
the head of whoever wrote
those two enigmatic words,
but first what was their gender
and their age. Was it someone
young enough to think of it
as just a mischievous prank?
Was it fuelled by anger and,
if anger, at what or whom?

And why were those two words placed
between the stylized figures
standing for man and woman

and just below "2m[etres]"
and the two-way arrow that's
there to keep the two apart?

Was it perhaps rebellion?
Does it mean, *No way are YOU*
(borough council, government,
persons in authority)
going to tell ME not to touch
my man (or boy, girl, woman,
whichever one's in question)?

Or just an indication
of fatigue with distancing?
If so, then who's it aimed at?
Whose expected to respond
to this imperative, and
what are they supposed to do?

Anger? Arrogance? Or else
the distressing evidence
of someone, male or female,
    who really was in pain?

June 9th, 2020, AH

A vision in early June

With the world turned upside down,
I blink with surprise —
look — *cherries on trees!*

June 11th, 2020, JP

Normal life

We walk about the streets
and talk to people who aren't there,
scarcely noticing the ones who are.

Briefly, social distancing changed that.
You just can't keep your distance
from people you don't see.

Now that it's relaxing . . . Give us an inch,
we take a mile. Contact sports I see
already in the parks,

and people congregate —
those sunny crowded weekend beaches.
Let's hope we'll get away with it . . .

Now that it's relaxing, our behaviour
reverts to normal, and strangers
start to disappear from view.

June 11th, 2020, AH

Domestic problem

(*Domestic* — not *Domestos* — problem
but confusion at the highest level
may be involved here too.)

For weeks now we've been unable
to find the particular type
of cellulose-sponge-backed scrubbers
that we like to use on pans.

I think it's not impossible
(there *are* certain precedents)
that the DOH has requisitioned
the nation's entire supply,
having failed to distinguish
between *scrubs* and *scrubbers*.

At least that will have kept
the manufacturers in business
and we can hope one day to find
our scrubbers in the stores again.

June 13th, 2020, AH

DOH = the UK government's Department of Health.

Good, better, worst

Our track-and-trace system,
billed by Boris as "world-beating",
needs to improve, the Chair
of the service itself acknowledges.

But from "world-beating"
where is there to go? What room
for improvement is there?
Best in the Universe?
Or just the Solar System?

Meanwhile the WHO
advises the UK
not to ease Lockdown any further
until its track-and-trace system
is "robust and effective".

"World-beating" but not "robust"?
"World-beating" but not "effective"?
"Robust and effective" sounds
good enough — I'd settle for that.
World-beating's not of much concern,
but then I'm not a politician.

Beat the World sounds suspiciously
akin to Make Britain Great Again —
and at a time when Churchill, tainted
by well-documented racist views,
is now in protective isolation
        on his plinth.

June 15th, 2020, AH

Covid exile

No planes and no trains —
she's locked out of her homeland.
Think how that must feel!

June 17th, 2020, JP

The bench (a dream)

I was sitting alone on a seaside bench;
a young man approached and boldly said,
"You look so old — ancient émigré or refugee?"

Nonplussed, I slowly raised myself to go.
I turned and read the small brass plaque:
IN LOVING MEMORY OF . . . Yes . . . *me* . . .

June 18th, 2020, JP

Mind the Gap
(Tell me lies about the NHS / Corona)

Mind the gap
  Between smiling for the nurses who pop things in and out
  Who bless you through your curses your terrors and your doubt
  Mind the gap between the waiting room and the ITU
  Between the easy listening and the ventilator blues
    Between the social distancing and the mortal breath
    Between the mask and pathogens that insinuate your death

Mind the gap
  Between rich and poor and white and black
  Between those craven lies and those cold corona facts
  Between the happy clapping outside your front doors
  Between thanking the NHS and keeping nurses poor
    Between duplicitous bulletins on your TV at five
    And the trauma on the front line of keeping us alive

Mind the gap
  Between a cold statistic and a croaking breath
  The agony of drowning, the moment of your death
    No hand to hold you, unwitnessed and unblessed
      No one to hear your last goodbye, no final tenderness
Mind the gap
  Between Intensive Care and the intensive carelessness
  Between the cutting and the killing of Nye Bevan's NHS

 Mind the gap
  Between 'the science' and the politician's stealth
  Between the truth and the minister of health
    Between his preaching 'civic duty' and stifling cheap mirth
    Between his rictus sadness and his cancelled smirk
    Between the ring fencing and the culling of care homes

It's a ring a ring o' roses and it's dying all alone

Mind the gap
  Between the unlocking of a lock down to keep the people sweet
  Between the beer and skittles on Bournemouth's sunny beach
  Between a dizzy dance of death between those winding sheets

Tell me lies about the NHS
  Get them in my head
  You say you want to save it
  Stop cutting it to shreds
  Tell me lies about corona
  And the 60,000 dead.

June, 20th, 2020, IW

ITU = Intensive Therapy Unit. Alternative names are
Critical Care Unit (CCU) and Intensive Care Unit (ICU).

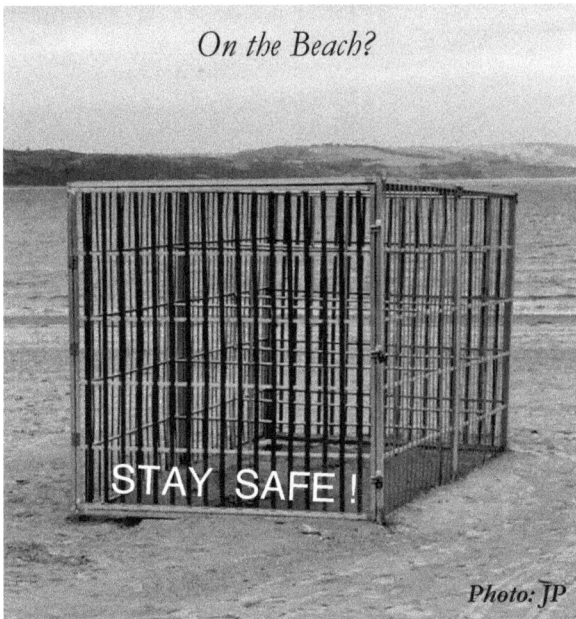

On the Beach?

STAY SAFE !

Photo: JP

The Cove House Inn, Portland

The Press called it "Suicide Sunday" —
in some places it was possibly so.
On Portland there were other attractions
— the wind had the force of a gale.
The pub had only just opened,
with a limited choice in the casks.
Outside, bench-tables were empty,
So I went in and ordered a pint.
All the barmen were sporting black masks.
When I tried to elbow open the door,
to watch the wild waves hit the shore,
the foam on my Guinness went flying,
stout and ale had flooded the floor.

July 5th, 2020, JP

Passenger Locator Form, Corfu Airport

The first flight, from Birmingham,
was saluted with a water arch.
Two days later, our packed flight from Bristol,
was welcomed by the PLF police.
The coded number on the form I carried
was surely not assigned at random —
I'd been profiled for my age and gender.
They directed me down a roped-off lane
for the dreaded COVID test.

I'm sitting here on Sunday
in self isolation,
listening to the church bells toll,
hoping I won't get a call
to report in with others
who are apparently "positive"
for an unwanted holiday
in the government's exclusive
COVID quarantine hotel.
But I *know* that I'm negative . . .

July 17th, 2020, JP

It's Not Just All in Your Head

One week before the covering
of mouth and nose
became mandatory
(in enclosed places)
I drifted out of Lockdown
into town
to buy a paper
with my homemade mask.

No one else in the shop
was wearing one.
No one actually *stared*
but I got some startled looks
as if I'd brought the virus in with me
to contaminate the town.

It was hard not to feel conspicuous
looking like Halloween
or hypochondriac, far-fetched,
showing off, compliant too soon?
Misinformed? I hurried on.

And reached the rows
of front page headlines on display.
HERE were featured masks on faces
FOR EVERYONE'S PROTECTION
Why wait? I wondered.

Will we be recognizable?
Speak clearly or just mumble?
Will I wear mine wrong-sided?
Will my spectacles steam up?

Being asked at check-out
"Are you OK?" took on extra meaning.
I nodded but did not attempt to say
"Yes . . . Thanks . . . Are you?"

July 17th, 2020, AR

*The Devil's Advocate
and the Coronavirus Pandemic*

A cynical friend, somewhat concerned
about his nearest and dearest,
and vulnerable rellies,
shocked me when speaking of the pros and cons,
of the contagious virus and a *population cull*;
of the benefits to lawyers, insurers —
more work for him and his legal colleagues,
for actuaries with their algorithms,
actuarial ages, risk assessments,
changes to mortality tables,
revised predictions, lower life-spans,
reduced pension pay-outs;
herd immunity — *and* fewer beds blocked.

July 25th, 2020, JP

Corfu opens up

It's worse in Spain,
but as the crowds arrive on Corfu,
every plane-load brings new cases.
I listen to the newscasts,
watch the carefree, uncovered faces.
The latest spreader's in Arillas,
in the north-west of the island;
I'm reminded that I didn't wear a mask
when chatting to a friend from there,
nor when a lady came to cut my hair.
It seemed rude to ask
that she should put on hers,
as we were out on the veranda.
I'm scolded by my daughter
skyping from America.
Another scare.
"It's everywhere!"

August 5th, 2020, JP

Corfu Friends

Jim and I have been meeting up with some of our Corfiot friends, to swim and talk and to put the world to rights. Recently, a former neighbour, now aged twenty (a night bird who'd come to stay from Athens), developed a fever and a cough, caught from a cousin, it would seem. He reported to a clinic, tested positive for Covid. Now our friends must stay at home — they're both confined, in quarantine. They've telephoned each contact, every person that they've seen wherever they've been since their nephew arrived. We only met them in open spaces or chatted in the sea; we thought we didn't need to cover faces.

Now two young Corfiot cricketers are sick, and the teenage daughters of someone else we know well. The transmission rate is doubling daily.

We've had a good innings up to now, some might say.

August 11th, 2020, MSP

Consider the handshake

All the ways we never thought
that casual touch could disappear —
from formal greeting one to one
to hands' embrace, held close, once dear —
the transformed mime of how we, thoughtless, touched.
Handshake diplomat to diplomat
step forward with a modest bow,
handshake greets the doctor,
handshake greets the friend,
the rough, the callused worn warm grip,
the unlined fine-tipped fingers formed,
the cool, thin, or the florid soft,
handshake says yes, affirms the self,
greets an elder, greets your peer.
Old etiquette: a kiss would be too much (too French)
a kiss on the mouth too familiar,
let her move first, if you're the man.
With a man, a solid grip, eyes meet, assess the neutral ground
through manners that have stood the test of time,
customs not yet gender free.
But now we are consumed by viral fear
encircled in these spheres with muffled breath
hands gloved, perhaps the fingertips compressed
palpate the skin, a hose, a line, through nitrile blue at best.

September 3rd, 2020, AGD

Grim prospects — autumnal Monday
(Corfu, September 2020, just before
returning to the UK)

The sea is quite flat;
my mood is low. Season's end.
Why bother to swim?

With hindsight I see —
I've wasted many summers
on pebbly beaches.

What a way to end our days —
in fear of more waves
or of fighting for breath . . .

Late September 2020, JP

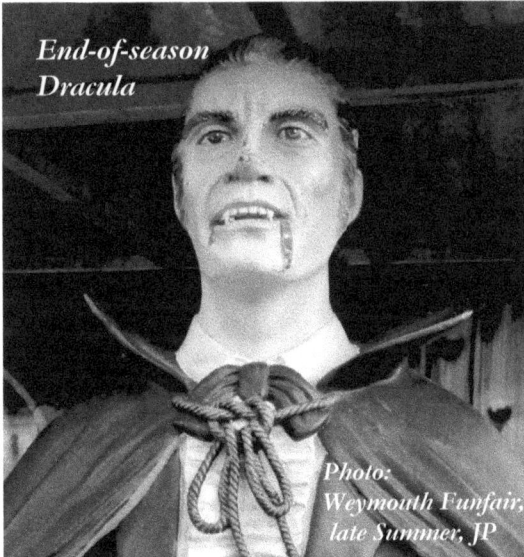

End-of-season
Dracula

Photo:
Weymouth Funfair,
late Summer, JP

115

Generation or gender?

I listened to *The Moral Maze*
on Radio 4 the other night.
One topic: the divide between
the generations — had it been
exacerbated by the current
Covid-19 pandemic?
But much of the discussion turned
on large-scale politics.

I noted that only the women
among the panellists
and "expert witnesses"
talked of co-operation,
while on the whole the men believed
free-market competition
(left free of state restraint)
would sort the whole mess out . . .
eventually. One even blamed
the Welfare State for many
of our present ills.
It does seem clear
we can't be safe as long as most
of the decisions that affect our lives
are made by men (or would-be manly
types like Thatcher and Patel).

October 23rd, 2020, AH

National Covid Memorial Wall, London. Photo: December 2022, JP
Other images of the wall on pages 123, 158–160, 174 and 189.
For information see page 158.

October 31, 2020: Boris Jonson announces a second Covid Lockdown for England,
to begin on 5 November and end on 2 December. (Still from BBC TV)

Thankless Job? No Thanks!

It's evening early.
Odd, this time of day
like candles lit in daylight.
The streets are deadly quiet
Cars parked up empty now.
Families seal themselves

indoors, plates clatter.

The Variety Show
starts at five for six p.m.
Sharp knives, peeling skins,
spills, spins, cutting boards,
steam and smoke alarms
produce two veg, meat and gravy.

Seems to take no time
to wolf it down.
Then what's for pudding?
Leftover cake please, to have
to hold and eat it too.
(Moldy old thing!)

Would be a luxury
to skip a meal
or step outside
and scoff a sandwich.
A little lost in thought
perhaps a little lonely.

Or take the family
out to eat
would be a treat
to find an open cafe!

November 10th, 2020, AR

The Quick and the Dead

We went down to Yeovil town to the crema-Tory-um
We rehearsed our little speeches for that brute emporium
When we said them in the service
  We mumbled through our masks
  We mumbled them to no one and a cancer corpse.

"Be quick!!" the Reverend had urged
  "Fifteen minutes max!"
  "No more fucking lockdowns!"
   The Convict too had urged
   "Let the bodies pile up high!
    Get those bodies burned."

You were snug in a pretty basket in a laundered dress
With lilacs and with lavender and your burnished tresses
At your side some Heaney and some lovely flowers wild
  You looked still like Ava Gardner with a Giaconda smile

Someone pressed a button for some brief and dying airs
"Abide with me", we mimed in tears and then a bit of Bach
We zoomed through our speeches he charged through his prayers
  Hell-bent to finish them he caught us unawares

Then the rev said something about the passing of the soul
Yours passed behind a curtain along some clunking rails
  It might be passing or transmigrating to on high
  It went into that furnace and you were lost in light

We walked into the mortal air, tried to avert our gaze
  We saw the next coffin and another thin cortege
  Quick! Boys! Bring out your bodies!
  Quick! Boys! Bring out your Dead!

Got to get them burned up just like the Convict said.

We went down to Yeovil town to that crema-Tory-um
Said some words that no one heard to no one and a corpse
We went down to Yeovil town to that crema-Tory-um
Wham bang thank you mam! Fifteen minutes maximum!
Fifteen minutes max!

November 12th, 2020, IW

Bread and circuses

The Second Wave's upon us.
Predictable. Indeed predicted
all along by those who understand
such things — those whose advice
our governments follow only
when it seems to suit their muddled aims.

The summer relaxation —
tourism must at all costs survive
and everyone must have a holiday,
even though the virus wouldn't,
and many were too destitute,
too short of food, to even think of it.

And now there's the imperative
of Christmas family get-togethers.
Masked and bumping elbows
beneath the mistletoe?
I hardly think so. We're clearly crackers
with our foolish mottos and our paper crowns.

November 18th, 2020, AH

Notification of Exceptional Movements of Citizens

*(adapted from the instructions for using
a Greek Government app during Lockdown)*

1. Going out to a pharmacy or a doctor. Please press ONE if you are looking for a cure, a healer or a soothsayer.

2. Going out shopping for essentials. Please press TWO if you are going out to look for your Being-In-The-World, the quintessence, the marrow, or your Own True Self.

3. Going out to a Government Office or a Bank. Please press THREE if you need something from the Vault where your virtual and paper-self are temporarily stored.

4. Going out to offer help to people in distress or to accompany students to school. Please press FOUR if you have a compassionate heart but DO NOT exceed the time-limits. If you do it too often, it may be seen as suspicious and you may be fined.

5. Going to a funeral, a wedding or a baptism or, in the case of divorced parents, going to communicate with their children in accordance with the law. Please press FIVE to undertake any of the above, which in the present circumstances all have the same taste and all feel the same.

6. Going a short distance from your place of residence for brief personal exercise or the needs of a pet. Please press SIX if you need to kiss, to hug, to cry or make time stop in any way. You can take your dog with you. Dogs are known to be good companions in Hades or the Elysium.

January 7, 2021.
866 Co-citizens Con-taminated, 27 Co-citizens Co-dying. Everybody else is fine. Homicides, femicides, deaths by war and hunger appear to have magically ceased in the face of this Co-predicament.

January 7th, 2021, ILM

National Covid Memorial Wall, London. Photos: December 2022, JP
Other images of the Wall on pages 117, 158–160, 174 and 189.
For information see page 158.

A jab in time saves lives?

When the call came, it took me by surprise
though only an hour before
I was trying to convince my worried wife.
"It will come soon," I told her, more in
hope than in expectation.
"You always say that," she said,
"always so positive, so bloody optimistic."
So when the call came I tried to
absorb the information
that might change our lives.
"A week today," said the voice,
"you at 12.18, your wife at 12.21."
So precise, but it was one bus
that we were not going to miss.
My brain quickly does the maths.
One minute to say goodbye
to the last patient.
One minute to welcome me
and perform the task.
One minute to clear the decks
before my wife is next.
I inform my wife, clutching my phone.
"It's Sandy from the practice,
she has got some good news."
"You are winding me up," she says,
"you are always winding me up."
"No, I'm not," I reply, "this time
it really is genuine."
In those three minutes, two
lives will be partially restored
not completely perhaps, but
a new freedom will be born,

a chance to get back some normality.
Our flattened lives may take on
a few more hills and challenges.
I imagine the moment. A voice
will say: "This should not hurt you,"
as I hold out my left arm.
A syringe will be produced
and vaccine will pour into
my vein and a plaster will
be placed on the spot.
And in those three minutes
two lives will take on
a new meaning, new hope.
Who knows? That tiny jab
May save two lives.
Such a feeling of anti-climax
but such a feeling of relief.

January 20th, 2021, MA

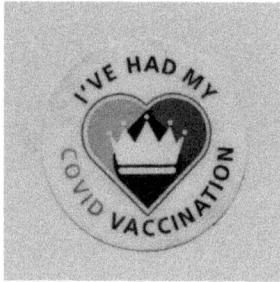

Well, the first shot of AstraZeneca, that is,
and in the Excel Centre, so it should be good.

The grey cord shirt that I was wearing — the material
was much too thick, the left sleeve wouldn't roll up high
enough, and so the nurse asked me to take it off.

If I'd anticipated this I might have worn
a different T-shirt, fond though I have always been
of this affectionate insinuation from
my elder daughter — birthday present years ago,
now fraying at the neck, mysterious yellow stains.
I like the label too, with *ACTIVE* in large letters,
LARGE in small — still, I like to think, a reasonable
description of the wearer.

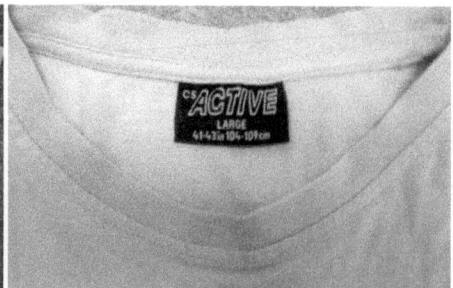

Tactfully the nurse
(who couldn't see the label) made no comment on
THE PLOT, but, the job done, peeled off a little sticker —
a heart with overlapping chambers and a crown —
and carefully applied it to the left-turn arrowhead.
I put my shirt back on, the sticker lost to view.

I wouldn't want to wear my nice round badge in public.
Some might be jealous or resentful, or might think
I wanted to show off my age. I might become
a target for the anti-vaxxers — what a fate!

But they're the ones, of course, who've really LOST THE PLOT.

January 23rd, 2021, AH

The sublime and the ridiculous
are not so far apart

Writing this morning to a friend,
I mentioned, just in general terms,
how different the world feels now
compared with how it felt six months ago,

and even more so, looking back
a year — the first of February
of twenty-twenty, the word "Covid"
not yet a part our vocabulary.

And then a line — or so I thought —
out of Zhivago's poem "Hamlet"
entered my mind. Perhaps the link
— the missing *link* — could have been "isolation"

and then an image that had vanished
even before I noted it —
a glimpse of Lara and Zhivago
in isolation at Varykino.

The house, the snow outside, the night,
wolves howling near and Lara scared,
the candle on the table burning,
Zhivago writing as their time runs out.

The misremembered line his Hamlet
speaks, as I wrote it down, was this:
"I step out onto the stage and
wonder what is to happen in my lifetime"

. . . conflating two lines, adding "wonder",
as I discovered when I checked,
once I'd retrieved *Doctor Zhivago*
from a large pile of books beside the bed.

In it, was a bookmark, a card
that must have come with some device
for hanging up inside a wardrobe
to stop the clothes moths ravaging the clothes.

Some dubious English, for it also
"free stands in rooms all around the home",
and some uncertain syntax in
the words END OF LIFE INDICATOR REFILL.

Few indicators yet of when
we'll be able to refill
our lives — well, those of us not yet
too late for REFILL, at the END OF LIFE.

February 1st, 2021, AH

Brave cowards

We're all like astronauts
on missions to outer space.
That's the way life is,
each time we climb out of bed.

Undated, JP

In Memoriam Faysal Mikdadi

SPRING DAFFODILS

William-like *I wandered lonely as a cloud*
that floats on high over our downs
reflecting on loves lost
some regained
a few maintained.
Many were loved, hated, despised
and a few dreaded — all beyond me now
for they are dead
awaiting my arrival
as I walk dragging my train
of three score and ten and more.
Contentedly maudlin in favoured solitude
wondering; when all is done
what will be . . . preferring not to know.
My inner eye searched for hope
when my outer landed on
a *host of daffodils* — large-cupped
giving self-love a new beauty.
Narcissus as a human
self loves and self immolates
but my landscape of Narcissi
fills me with joy and hope
of a Spring rebirth soon
and life continuing even after.

February 2nd, 2021, Faysal Mikdadi

Faysal Mikdadi, the Academic Director of the Thomas Hardy Society, "passed away in the morning of Thursday 5th August 2021. It was not expected." Although it is Wordsworth whom Faysal invokes in this poem, in feeling it is more akin to Hardy. On the facing page, the extracts from a poem of Hardy's and the photo of the monument in Poundbury Cemetery on which its closing words appear are offered as a tribute to Faysal, followed by five poems of mourning by Susan Walpole and Julian Nangle.

from "Nature's Questioning" by Thomas Hardy (1840–1928)

When I look forth at dawning, pool,
    Field, flock and lonely tree,
    All seem to gaze at me
Like chastened children sitting silent in a school . . .

Upon them stirs in lippings mere
    (As if once clear in call,
    But now scarce breathed at all) —
"We wonder, ever wonder, why we find us here! . . ."

In the Poundbury Cemetery, Dorchester

LIFE AND DEATH ARE NEIGHBOURS NIGH
THOMAS HARDY

Photo: JP

Thus things around. No answerer I . . .
    Meanwhile the winds, and rains,
    And Earth's old glooms and pains
Are still the same, and Life and Death are neighbours nigh.

131

I LOVED YOU ONCE

I loved you once
and once turned to many more
days and nights of wild love,
deep, sure, lasting, longing.
No separation on earth
until, one day, you were gone
in a flicker of an eyelid,
a stop in time, barely a second
when your heart stopped its
mighty beat and your soul
departed on a breath of air.

You were so cold, so cold before you left;
I couldn't warm your hand, held still in mine,
still strong, with skin soft as a baby's;
too soon this mortal coil ends its
time, and a light goes out on earth.
Yet, in that same moment, a soul
is lit in another universe, another
realm which I know exists but cannot reach
for now. You will wait with patience to
guide my soul to you when my eyes close
for the final time and my body sleeps
that longest sleep of all.

And so, although we are in separate realms
for now, our hearts remain entwined and
I am become your eyes, your ears, your voice.
Your lost voice, which even now,
whispers comfort in my times of

direst need, when tears fall and sobs —
wrenched from my broken heart
with the missing of you.

Susan Walpole

OUR STORY

I sit down at the cricket pitch
It calms my racing thoughts
I feel close to you here in the quiet
Of an evening when I've walked
My daily walk.
You appear in the guise of a magpie.
Borrowed feathers cladding your naked soul
I know it is you by the strutting back and forth
And the inquisitive stare whilst I rest above the pitch.
You always stared so, a life-long habit of observation
Trying to understand the people that you watched
You wove stories about their person,
Little histories of little lives.
I feel you now trying to write my story after you.
Too soon, my love, too soon.

My story is on hold as I sift through our story
Trying to make sense of how it ended all too soon
The love and laughter and deepest inner thoughts
We shared. Private still. Perhaps forever.

I watch now as you did for all our years
I think of how even the smallest meanest life has value
As your life did.
It is the little things that get to me
A look you used to give when you didn't understand
A word, a phrase uttered
A laugh out loud or a quiet kiss
Arms around each other just because we could
And sometimes just because of need
To feel beloved above all else.

I will write my story in good time, beloved man,
But for now, my love,
Too soon, too soon . . .

Susan Walpole

THE PERFECT DAY

The perfect day is not contiguous
but comes from other days' moments
joining together into glorious memory.

The first espying, the first kiss, the first
"I love you" all conspire to create that perfect day.

A quiet meal of favourite foods with
discussions on life and all things beyond ourselves;
sunshine in the garden during Autumn cool,
snatched snippets of other peoples' lives,
holidays abroad, Paris, Florence and Neuchâtel,

silly cycle rides, long walks, trips across the water,
Morat/Murten and 'Mozart's' tea room;
fondu in Bern, a glass of Swiss wine, filets de perche
in Auvernier, skinny fries and fresh green salad;
croissants in Paris in the early morning,
le chocolat chaud, bitter and dark,
Le Louvre and La Giaconda
casting spells with her enigmatic smile;
opera in Florence, soul-searchingly searing;
real pizza in La Giardino di Boboli, the Uffizi,
Veneziano's Virgin and Child, Botticelli's Birth of Venus,
da Fabriano's Adoration of the Magi,
perfection assaulting our senses;
Ponte Vecchio, dripping with gold, a cameo brooch
purchased with love from you to me . . .

Tramping through fields close to home,
eating English strawberries, juicy red staining fingers,
strolling by the river, a picnic lunch at a hidden table,
the three trees circled in "Bathsheba's field",
sheep wandering woolly to lunch on lush green grass;
young people relaxing by the river, giggling, flirting,
stealing innocent kisses as only they can.

These are the moments of a perfect day,
nestling in the recesses of the mind,
surging to consciousness, living again, dispelling sadness
when days seemed dark and
loneliness sat heavy on shoulders hunched . . .

Susan Walpole

THIS MAGICAL RAIN

(I.M. FAYSAL MIKDADI)

What happens to the rain
falling
on the flowers of my imagination?
Will it come again
so I can drink in
your loss, set in train
thoughts
brought by this tunnelling pain?
To recognize all you gave me
I must relive our conversations
stolen from the daily round of life
in cafes, pubs and coffee bars,
in the comfortable chairs
at The Duchess of Cornwall
and the Gallery on the Square
where you talked, intimately,
of secret messages from your sister
still stuck in Beirut
before moving on
to tell me my latest poem
stood tall with others
already included
in your fast expanding file
for my new book.
But where's the rain gone
that waters the creation of such
beautiful friendship
and meets the thirst
for love and
recognition

all exiles need —
where's it all gone, this magical rain,
will it come again
can it ever come again?

Julian Nangle

I FIND MYSELF IN 2022

I find myself in 2022, whilst you
are forever in 2021.
This panics me more than you will ever know.
Don't look back, they tell me all the time.
Go forward, be brave, strike out on your own
        for your mind's sake.
I cannot let you go as if you never were, my life, my love.
You come still in my dreams and
quiet moments and we laugh
and talk as we were wont to do
all those days and nights of our shared past.
Your voice sings gently in my ear
of love we'll always share.
My heart binds firmer to your soul and carries you with me
for comfort on the lonely days
I now endure.

Susan Walpole

———— • ————

Are you thinking of dying?

Death is rarely something you can organize —
your *own* death, I mean. What happens after,
even what becomes of your own body,
that you can control, can specify it,
set it down in your last will and testament.

But not the event itself — the non-event,
end of all events, for you — unless of course
you decide to orchestrate the thing yourself,
play the role of your own executioner.

Death by misadventure, death from natural causes?
The first comes, by definition, unannounced.
The second may (a heart attack, a
fatal stroke) or may not (a lingering illness,
slow decline) rule out all preparation.

Many would not choose to see it coming,
prefer to imagine dying in their sleep
with no warning, no foreknowledge, no knowledge
even in the moment. When they turn the light off,
close their eyes each night, aren't they a little anxious?

Medical procedures, with, or else without, your
own consent, may keep your poor heart pulsing
for a little while beyond its natural term. At best
you're on death row, your own prison governor,
the timing, within limits, in your hands.

If you're rich — that's very rich, or superrich —
you can take a gamble on cryonics, but
don't forget to say goodbye to friends who

can't afford it. Rip Van Winkle, Sleeping Beauty,
your own fairy tale is waiting in a world
where perhaps you won't be wanted, which you won't be
able to inhabit, and which may well never come.

As for me, I would prefer to see death coming
with my thoughts and my emotions still intact.
To have time — days, weeks — for my farewells.
Time to weep with others in advance of my demise,
share their mourning for their loss of me,
mine for my loss of them — and of the whole universe,
which, for all its horrors, I have loved so much,
loved, that is, the very little of it I have known.

That's the kind of death so many've been so
cruelly deprived of this past year
as the virus rendered them untouchable
to all their familiars beyond the care-home walls
or outside the hospital environment.

Admiration knows no bounds — *my* admiration
for those doctors, nurses, carers who have grasped
the grim nature of such deprivation, who've been
stand-ins for their locked-out family and friends,
held the hands of strangers, whispered soothing words
as they watched light fading from their patients' eyes,
then drawn up the sheets to cover their still faces.

February 6th, 2021, AH

Be-Bop-a-Lula

Green Lanes and Aden Grove
London N16

I'm not sure this Corona sign's
The best way in these scary times
To pull folks in and anyway
The pub's locked down and we're locked out
Gotta wait for our Corona shout —
Extra!   Premier!   Familiar!   Light!

There's Gene Vincent on the hanging sign
That's him too above the corner door
He's the monarch of THE MONARCH — Right?

Be-Bop-a-Lula she's my baby
She's the one with the flying feet
Corona bops around the store
Be-Bop-a-Lula I don't mean maybe
She's the one that's got me beat
Corona gives me more more more

Let's rock again now! No, that ain't right
Gotta wait till *Corona's* Light Light Light

February 10th, 2021, AH

One day, two scenarios
(for Maria)

One day this warm hand I'm holding will turn quite cold,
and I'll feel in your wrist no sign of a pulse.

One day this large hand you're squeezing will turn numb,
and the fingers will fail to unlock my phone.

We need no prophet to tell us this.

Hold on. I'm calling.

24th of February 2021, JP

*Jim and Maria
in Oxford in 2016
(above)*

*in Prague, winter
1987 or '88 (right)*

*Maria died in
May 2022 (see
pages 175–186)*

The writing on the walls

All these graffiti have appeared within
the last few days, all on a route I often take —
on every second or third day at least.

It's only a few minutes' walk from
Lavell Street — "Where your inner child gone" —
to Aden Terrace — "Fear is their only medicine".
You don't need a graphologist to tell you
both are the work of one graffiti artist.

Though the tail of the y in "your" is straight,
the closed curl on the g of "gone"
matches that of the y in "only";
the way the letters crowd together
making contact where they shouldn't;
small capital R, twice in each location;

script height the same; the same blue paint on white —
the canvas in Lavell street ready-made,
an-end-of-terrace wall rendered and painted
to just above the ground-floor ceiling height,
in Aden Terrace, carefully prepared:
eight concrete fence planks neatly primed in white.

But what's this all about? Are these
pandemic messages? What's the disease
that "Fear" can cure? Or maybe cannot cure
if irony's intended, and contempt
for those in charge with nothing else to offer?
And, if not, who are *they* who might
administer the "*their* only medicine"?
Or are they those with nothing else
with which to treat themselves?
Is "Fear" the feeling that informed the writer?
No, surely not, at least not that alone,

but anger — it's an accusation.
And "Where your inner child gone", that too
could be an accusation — words of one
who feels that he (I sense it's *he* not *she*)
has still retained his inner child and holds
himself superior to the grim
and heartless others who surround him,
or whom he passes daily in the street
and sees wrapped up inside their own concerns.
And here perhaps, more than in the third-person
statement concerning "Fear", one senses fear
and inner insecurity behind
all the bravado of the question.

In Aden Terrace we also find a single-word
graffito in what is almost certainly
a different hand: ΕSCAPE , , ,

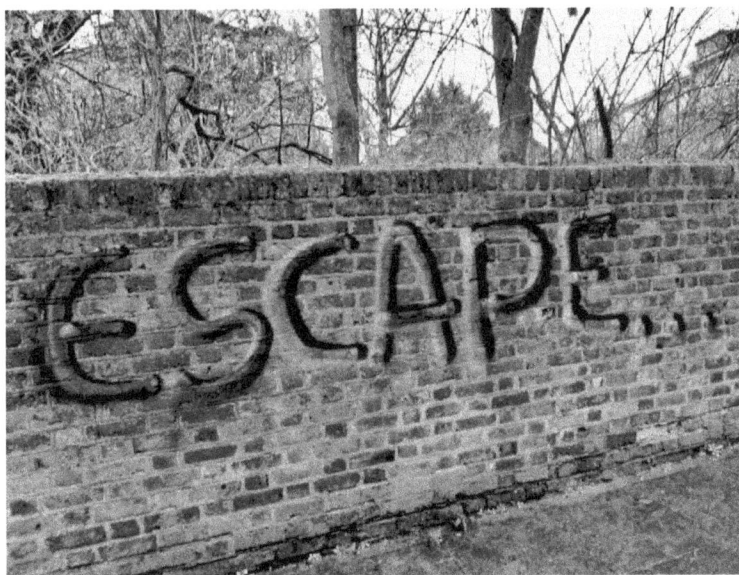

with its four trailing commas,
the first attached to E the others free; all capitals,
with two quite different Es, the first one Greek,
or hinting at the euro sign. The letters in
two colours, double lined, the darker lines
are blue, the lighter green — crude shadow style.

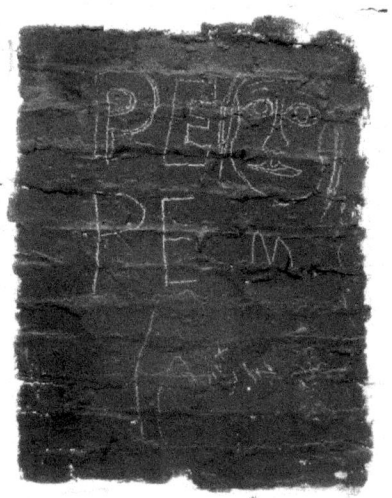

And only a few yards away in white
on black some letters and a face.
Note that the first P here
is also shadow style. So could this be
the face, the somewhat troubled face —
young, I assume, and maybe female as the hair
perhaps suggests — of She who's longing to . . .
ESCAPE , , , ? From what? To where? And How?

And then "PE" twice. What's this?
Repeated initials or PEPE —
not usually a name for girls.

In Aden Terrace some weeks
later the writings can still be seen.
In Lavell Street, though,
the pointed question
"Where your inner child gone"
didn't long survive; within a week
was painted over white,
almost but not quite matching
the original, the background white.
Maybe several coats.
The writing is still there of course

beneath the paint, a ghostly presence
which can just be seen in certain lights.
Still there, like repressed fear,
emotion, thought, but now no longer

"desecrating" someone's property.
Economy of paint produced
not one single rectangle
but, following the pattern
of tall letters and descenders,
a complex rectilinear form.
That too is still discernible.

The roadworks are a different matter,
just coincidence — unless someone
is digging for their lost inner child.

January 14th and February 27th, 2021, AH

So much is over
(In memoriam Jill Poppy)

"You do these things alone."
"Give me the morphine"
was all that she said.

So much is over,
except for the tears,
except for the bluebells . . .

"So much is over"
months after the end
my grieving friend said.

March 6th, 2021, JP,
but largely composed of phrases from Ian Whitwham's emails.
See his poems on pages 26–27, 31, 106–107 & 120–121.

Trainee boxer

Off to buy the newspaper
A walk through the park, the day golden, iridescent
Ahead I saw a young man in vest and shorts
His arms muscled, glistening
Punching the air, boxing mode
His movements were swift, controlled, powerful
His concentration intense
Energy flew off him like sparks
He was not masked
I stopped, uncertain
I think I'll give you a wide berth, I said,
but it looks like really good exercise
He stopped, his concentration broken, and relaxed
He gave me a wide, gap-toothed smile
Yes it is actually, really good
I moved on

March 7th, 2021, FH

Remains

You there
Poet unrecognized
sifting, sorting private papers
some scribbled, some typed
keepsakes, scraps, momentary gems
of genius (words do that themselves).
There's time . . . you tell yourself.

then and there you start
a single volume of copied out
selections, remnants, remains.
An oeuvre slim enough to hide itself
in the bookshelf.

You burn the rest
like a pile of leaves
bleached by fire.
Ashes with no life left
of their own to be read.

All this, just in case
you are whisked away by Covid
to perish without distinction.

No ripple or ruffle
on water, sand or wind

March 23rd, 2021, AR

My Covid-19 Reading Year

(March 24th, 2020 – March 23rd, 2021)

My reading year began more earnestly, after Johnson had announced on March 23rd, 2020 that the country would begin a full National Lockdown from March 24th.

I have always been an avid reader and have regularly read at least a book a month for most of my life. My favourite reads were, and still are, Charlotte Brontë's *Jane Eyre* and Margaret Mitchell's *Gone with the Wind*. I had read both of these novels by the time I had turned twelve years old. Prior to that, I read as many books as I could get my hands on. Books were a godsend in many ways. They gave you worlds to escape to when the real world was not always as you wished it to be.

Many are the hours I have been curled up in a comfy chair, a warm bed or a seat in the garden avidly devouring another book. The words on the page took me to Caribbean islands, Russia, China, India, European countries, America North and South, or the wilds of Britain, through modern times, ancient times, medieval times and even the future. What I have noticed from these travels through these books is the continuity of human stories; what affected people in the past continues to affect us now and will, I think, affect us in the future too. Love, war, pestilence, jealousy, anger and despair will always be a part of our story through the ages.

Which books do I prefer? I am an eclectic reader and purchaser of books. History, literary criticism, novels, post-colonial works, poetry, drama and politics are all in my sights. I read pre-twentieth-century novels with as much joy as more modern novels. The same can be said of dramas and poetry. Sometimes it is easier to read from earlier times about those things which disturb us. Perhaps there is some safety in knowing that the event discussed is in the past and that these things no longer happen. A rather naïve attitude, I know, because history repeats and repeats and one wonders whether humans will ever learn from previous generations. However, without the hope that we will learn we could easily become very disenchanted with the world and make no effort to try and move forward.

I have read numerous lightweight novels this year; interspersing them with the heavier tomes of pre-twentieth-century authors. Edward Marston and his Railway Detective series have been enjoyable reads when I have not wanted to flex my brain too severely, as too Rebecca Tope's West Country murder series. In addition to these light fiction writers, I have journeyed my way through around twenty Christmas novels which definitely come under the heading of "frothy" reading and which provided a nice backdrop to the lead up to Christmas. Nothing too strenuous within their Christmassy covers — just old-fashioned twee love stories played out against the background of the Christmas season. Much more entertaining than Boris's announcements of "shall we, shan't we" Christmas gatherings which ultimately contributed to the horrendous time our hospitals have been suffering in this new year.

Enough of Boris! "Books and more books" is the antidote to a lockdown. You cannot go far wrong with a good book in your hands and a cosy chair in front of a log fire whilst the world is going mad around you. My year started with Richardson's *Clarissa*. An epic tome in every sense of the word. Its epistolary style, like Alice Walker's *The Color Purple*, added much urgency to the protagonist's situation and angst. It revealed a young lady who, feeling that she was the centre of her family, adored and respected by the "world", was far too naïve in her trusting of those around her not to manipulate her into situations that she could not manage effectively. There were times whilst reading this novel, when, as a modern reader, an urge to shake her was often felt and, as another woman, feeling emotionally overwrought at the sheer horror of what was happening to her as well as her own complicity and vulnerability in a society which would blame her rather than the male alone. How could someone be so blind as to think that family would do everything to protect one when a brother's wounded pride was at stake, a sister's romantic slight caused excessive jealousy of their parents' pleasure in her, and a man obsessed with forcing her into marriage specifically to aggravate her family by ruining her both physically and socially? We like to think in our very enlightened way that this kind of situation could not and does not happen in these days. Rivalry is alive and well in many families and society in general still!

Richardson's drawing of his characters provokes strong feelings despite being written in the eighteenth century. Perhaps it could be argued that it is because it was written so long ago and that, in reality, little in terms of the big themes of life change; their interpretation and presentation might change but the basic truths never change. This is the universality of writing. Little really changes across the years despite our thinking we are more civilised and better educated than people from years gone by.

Before I embarked on Vikram Seth's sweeping depiction of family and society in post-colonial India, *A Suitable Boy*, I read a series of novels by less well-known authors in the murder/mystery genre. Authors such as Frances Brody — *A Snapshot of Murder* — and Lorna Nicholl Morgan — *The Death Box*. Thank goodness for places like The Works where one can pick up cheaper novels in their "3 for £5" offers. Cheap enough for most people to indulge in, at the very least, light reading. These are also so cheap that they can be passed onto neighbours or friends who like to read but don't feel like they have the time to go book-buying.

Back to Seth's novel. I had begun to read *A Suitable Boy* several years ago and had put it to one side as it had not "grabbed" me after the first two to three chapters. I find this often happens when the book has been recommended and enthused over by another reader. Perhaps it is a subconscious perverseness that one had not "discovered" the book for oneself!

The reason I picked this novel up again was following the rather excellent BBC adaptation screened in July, 2020. I had read the reviews of the mini-series and my interest was piqued by critics who said that the novel was just too sweeping to ever be filmed and that this adaptation was only partially successful in grasping the scope of Seth's work. I respectfully disagree with those critics. I found the essence of India was beautifully captured, the actors were well chosen and played their parts sympathetically. I was captured by their performances.

As soon as the series ended, I visited my book shelves and retrieved the novel. Despite having previously read the first few chapters, I began again. This time the book captured my imagination. I could see and hear the characters in a way I had not done in my initial attempt at reading. At this point, I should say that I do not usually watch a screen adaptation of novels before reading them. I have always preferred to read a book and then see the film in order to allow my mind to engage with the characters first rather than have someone else's interpretation impose itself on me. As I used to tell my students, films of books or plays are one person's vision and developing your own vision first enables you to better critique what you see. This approach usually helps develop confidence in your own judgements. I hear you say now that I did not follow my own advice with *A Suitable Boy*. You are right of course but needs must in some circumstances! Had I not watched the mini-series I would never have gone on to complete my reading of a brilliant novel and would have lost out on a real gem of a book. Who could fail not to respond to Lata Mehra, her eventual husband Haresh Khanna, her scheming mother Rupa Mehra, her obnoxious and snobbish brother Arun Mehra and his unfaithful wife Meenakshi, Maan Kapoor and Saeeda Bai. Within this novel you have many of the themes covered by Jane Austen in her many novels dealing with how society marries off young women to suitable young men. The minutiae of society is beautifully detailed and acts as a splendid backdrop for Rupa's manoeuvring and machinations on her daughter's behalf.

Between these two epic tomes there was, once again, time to read something a bit lighter. E. M. Forster's *Howards End* served this purpose very well. An acutely observed study of the class war and the English character based around the lives of three families from different classes. Each class is drawn in all its idiosyncrasies as we follow the Schegels' dealings with a rich family (the Wilcoxes) and a poor family (the Basts.) There are, in my opinion, no likeable characters but there are characters who are deserving of our empathy. The Basts fall into this category. Forster draws them with a vicious eye which makes it feel like an overtly authorial intervention. In fact, Forster regularly interposes himself within the narrative; something which can be irritating at times because this reader prefers to be left to interpret the narrative for herself. The most appealing aspect of the novel for myself was actually the fact that the main characters are female and exert an influence over the male characters in similar ways to the usual male influence over female characters. This is not to say that male influence is completely absent, rather it is more subtle.

I should point out that this wander through my year of reading is not necessarily chronological in its listing. I don't think that this detracts in any way from what I am describing but you must be the judge of that.

Andrea Levy's *Small Island* was another enjoyable read. Again, in my view, a novel which has the feminine viewpoint at its front but does not exclude the male perspective either. Hortense and Queenie are wonderfully drawn in this exploration of the female experience of war and its aftermath, emigration and immigration from Jamaica, and the closed mind of small island racist society, both in Jamaica and in Britain. The growing relationship between Queenie and Hortense is documented through first person narrated chapters for each woman and eventually shows their growing respect for each other. Well worth the three cups of hot chocolate and the mini mince-pies retrieved from the freezer.

The list of reading goes on and on. The complete set of Morse entertained and got the brain ticking over trying to make sense of the little hints dropped casually within the pages as the stories developed. Closely followed by Christie's Poirot and his "little grey cells" carrying me along the Nile. Or through the buffet car of the Orient Express. Pure joy on a warm Spring afternoon with only the two of us, feet up and hands stretched across the arm of a chair in order that fingertips might touch but not intrude on the other's reading matter.

My annual favourite of *Jane Eyre* still touches my heart, as it did the first time I read it, at the tender age of ten years old. I am part way through it once more and still find myself annoyed with Mrs Reed for her unkind treatment of Jane, and even more annoyed that Jane did not have the courage of her love for Mr Rochester to flout Society's rules and just live with him.

As with all good things, sometimes you just feel the need to "mix it up a bit" and so, with this in mind, my attention inevitably turned to poetry. It is here, in the poets I love that Faysal and I disagree quite strongly. He loves Wordsworth and his "lonely clouds" and "daffodils". I cannot stand either! Many is the time I have rolled my eyes at the appearance of Mr Wordsworth. I get an over-whelming sense of irritation whenever Faysal picks him up. I am quite possibly in the extreme minority of people for this dislike, and so we have agreed to disagree on his worthiness rather than come to verbal blows over him.

I have however introduced him more properly to Emily Dickin-son, Anne Bradstreet and Langston Hughes, to name a few of my favourite poets. Of course, I must not overlook Thomas Hardy in this — especially as Faysal is a recent Academic Director of The Hardy Society! We were in the poetry group which met every third Wednesday of the month at Maxgate, until Lockdown prevented it. We were, thanks to technology, able to take the group online and every month we have requested members to email their poetry choices from Hardy and others to us and we have circulated them via Round Robin emails for members to enjoy. Will we ever meet face to face again?

I have read Margaret Beaufort's biography; a very interesting exploration of a powerful woman succeeding in a man's world. An exploration of Julian of Norwich was interesting. Norwich is my home city and it was interesting to read with this in mind. Anne Hathaway's biography was another joy picked up before Lockdown and on the pile of "to be read".

So many books read, so many waiting to be read. I wonder if I will be alive long enough to finish reading all the books I want to read. Do I need to have another Lockdown to keep reading? No, not really. Everyone should read and then read a bit more. What is this life if we do not read, do not learn from what we read and do not pass the love of reading on to our children and their children ad infinitum?

I have to stop now; Jane is calling me to finish her story . . .

March 24th, 2021, SW

The National Covid Memorial Wall

created by bereaved families

The hearts on this wall are in memory of our fellow citizens who have died since March 2020 with Covid-19 on their death certificates.

Every heart represents a person who was loved.

The wall belongs to us all, and we all have to share it. If you want to add an inscription to the wall in memory of someone whose life was lost to Covid-19, please abide by the original principles:

♥ **Please only take one heart for each person**

♥ **Find a freshly-painted heart and make your dedication**

♥ **Hearts should be similar in size and no larger than an adult hand**

The Friends of the Wall are a group of bereaved volunteers who maintain the memorial by removing graffiti, repeated inscriptions and re-painting fading hearts. All efforts are being made to maintain original dedications.

We can be contacted on Twitter at @CovidMemorialUK. Please get in touch if you would like to volunteer. Donations for the upkeep of this memorial can be made at nationalcovidmemorialwall.org

This Memorial Wall was inaugurated on March 29th, 2021 and is still being added to. There are now (September 2023) more than 220,000 hearts. It is located on the south embankment of the Thames in London, facing the Houses of Parliament. Other images of the wall on the next two pages and on pages 117, 123, 174 and 189. (Photos: December 2022, JP). See www.nationalcovidmemorialwall.org for information on its creation and maintenance, and on its future.

Mass psychosis?

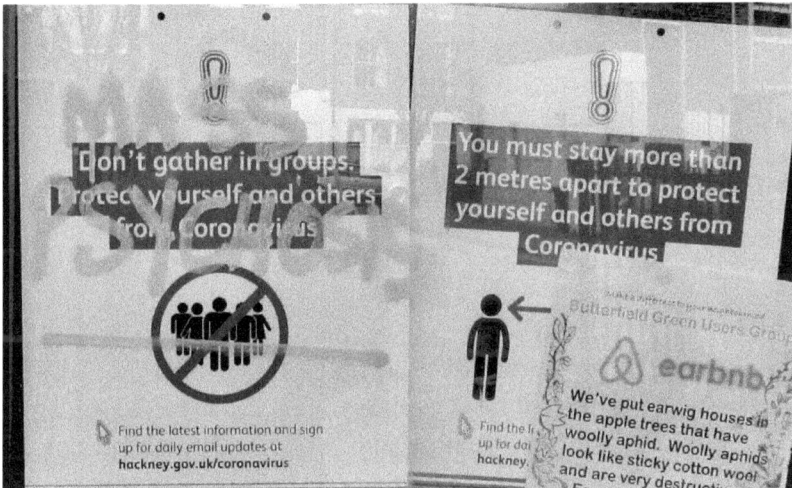

Is this a message from
some daft conspiracy theorist
who thinks we've all been duped
and made to fear a phantom epidemic;
and made, by fear, conformist to
the sinister instructions of our governments?

Or is it a prediction of
the outcome of our social distancing?

The first would be alarmist nonsense
betraying wilful ignorance,
reliance on the least reliable
and most disreputable sources of
        misinformation and deceit.

As for the second, yes, indeed,

there are so many people of all ages
severely disturbed now by isolation,
and then the millions of distraught bereaved.
But mass psychosis? No. The oldest can
remind us that the War was worse —
like any war no matter where or when.
And most of us can manage. We'll get by.

Maybe tomorrow I'll commit an act
of censorship — watching my back —
and wipe those white words off the glass.

Facebook, take note and follow suit.
Cite "freedom of expression" if you like
but those who lie, or pass on lies unchecked,
intending, or just causing, harm to others
are very far from having earned that freedom.

◆

I failed to carry out my act of censorship
and that left time for others to add comments,
to add new layers to the palimpsest.

The main one is a simple statement of the fact
that COVID KILLS!! — in fine red lines, the letters large,
COVID on top of MASS, and KILLS!! over PSYCHOSIS,
neat cancellation of the underlying phrase.
The layers now are red on white on white-on-red.

Written with much less confidence at bottom left,
difficult even at close quarters to make out,
a much less welcome message, DIE YOU BASTARDS,
suggesting by position and the angle
that it may be directed at symbolic people

gathered in a group inside their road-sign circle
with its oblique don't-do-it line,
itself already cancelled out perhaps
by that thick line that goes with MASS PSYCHOSIS.

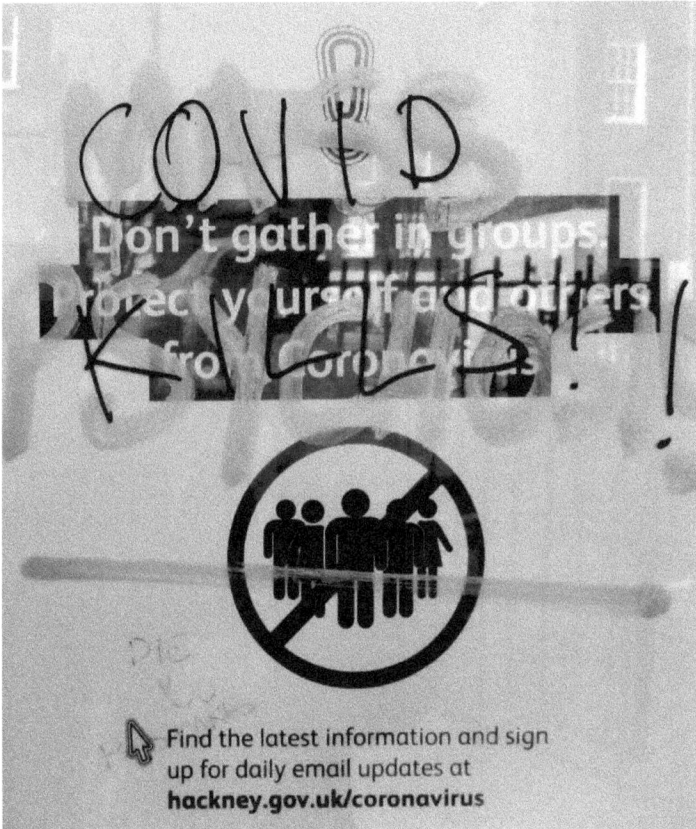

So here we are, instructed, sensibly,
to stay apart, protect ourselves and others,
accused of madness if we do, then warned of death,
and in the latest message told to die.

That wasn't quite the end of it, however.
Now six short strokes have transformed COVID
into GOVER and then NMENT's been added
with 1984 above (all red again),
taking us back, at least half way,
to MASS PSYCHOSIS, but with reason —
alluding to the new police powers bill
(one little step towards a fascist state,
Big Brother Boris and his Brutal Bobbies),
while, added maybe by a different hand,
the blood runs down from 8 and N and T.

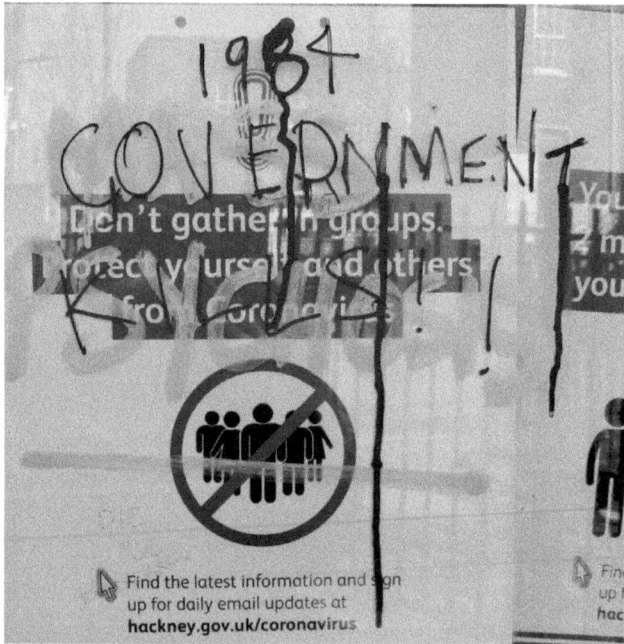

Butterfield Green, London N16
March 7th, 22nd and 29th, 2021, AH

Home Test for Corona Virus (a Greek approach)

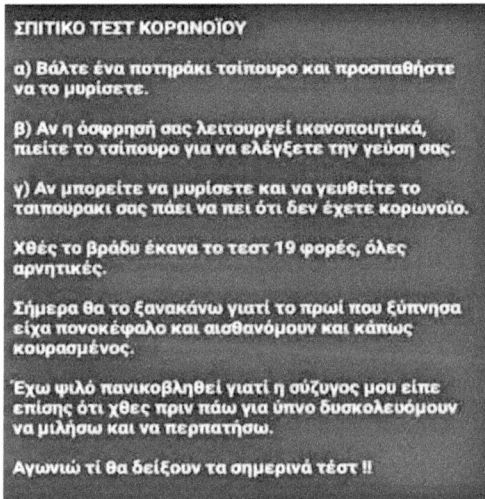

ΣΠΙΤΙΚΟ ΤΕΣΤ ΚΟΡΩΝΟΪΟΥ

α) Βάλτε ένα ποτηράκι τσίπουρο και προσπαθήστε να το μυρίσετε.

β) Αν η όσφρησή σας λειτουργεί ικανοποιητικά, πιείτε το τσίπουρο για να ελέγξετε την γεύση σας.

γ) Αν μπορείτε να μυρίσετε και να γευθείτε το τσιπουράκι σας πάει να πει ότι δεν έχετε κορωνοϊό.

Χθές το βράδυ έκανα το τεστ 19 φορές, όλες αρνητικές.

Σήμερα θα το ξανακάνω γιατί το πρωί που ξύπνησα είχα πονοκέφαλο και αισθανόμουν και κάπως κουρασμένος.

Έχω ψιλό πανικοβληθεί γιατί η σύζυγος μου είπε επίσης ότι χθες πριν πάω για ύπνο δυσκολευόμουν να μιλήσω και να περπατήσω.

Αγωνιώ τί θα δείξουν τα σημερινά τέστ !!

Posted on various social media sites since March 2021, found by JP

1) Take a small glass of whisky and try to smell it.

2) If your sense of smell is working satisfactorily, drink the whisky in order to test your sense of taste.

3) If you are able to smell and taste your shot of whisky that tells you that you do not have the Corona Virus.

Last night I did the test 19 times — all negative.

Today I am going to test again because this morning I woke up with a headache and was feeling rather tired.

I had a serious panic attack when my wife told me that before I went to sleep last night I had problems with speaking and walking.

I am very worried about what today's tests may show!!

The original refers to "tsipouro" for which "whisky" has been substituted. Translation, AH.

My Zoom Portraits

Making these iPad paintings fulfilled a dual purpose for me. I had several arranged meetings on Zoom with close friends and family who I was now — March 2020 — by Law unable to meet up with. So we chatted (sometimes we "shared a meal" together or even played games) and at each meeting I began to photograph the screen — just as a memory . . . then I thought, umm, maybe I'll use these photos to make paintings . . . and I asked them if they would mind if they became part of a project. Of course they didn't, and so it went on through the whole year and into 2021 — when at least for a few weeks we were able to actually meet again.

Making the paintings meant that I "spent a lot more time" with the friends, thinking about them in their familiar surroundings while I was concentrating on the paintings . . . So, more pleasure, or sometimes perhaps irritation or despair as one might have felt if we'd been together. A quite different experience from having a sitter for a portrait in the room with you.

March 2020 – April 2021, SFR

from
Linked-verse meditations

In parts of England
days before
the big relaxation
the Indian Variant is spreading.

In India itself
the sick are dying
in the streets
faster than their bodies can be burned.

May 13th, 2021, AH

I Spy

My little eyes are failing to spy.
My sight is beginning to blur.
What can I see? I won't tell a lie —
"It's something beginning with C . . .

Now you be *It.*"

"It's something beginning with D . . ."

September 6th, 2021, JP

168

ONS Covid-19 Infection Survey

"We know you're no longer with us but
your opinion
still means a lot."

October 15th, 2021, JP

ONS = the UK Office of National Statistics

Recurrent Covid nightmare
(virtual reality)

Each night in my dreams
I struggle with the Devil.
He comes in many forms and guises.
We fight in filthy stagnant ponds.
He grabs the wheel
while I'm driving.
We wrestle on hill forts
and in pools of slurry.

On hospital wards he's a doctor.
He tears off my oxygen mask,
or he hovers with a lethal injection.
He comes with stealth
like a nurse in the night.
I watch as he writes
DO NOT RESUSCITATE!
He can't wait. He's in a hurry.

October 31st, 2021, JP

Obstacles
to Mindfulness

I can't concentrate
on Homer.
It's not *The Iliad*
that's bad. It's just
that life is short.
And Boris makes
me mad.

November 30th, 2021, JP

Horror Scopes

Scorpio? Monkey?
Makes no difference.
I'm anxious all the time.

January 1st, 2022, JP

Taken short

Your heart could stop
at any time.
Better smell those roses.

Undated, JP

Unlocked language

Change from *pandemic*
to *endemic*. Play with words.
It's just a game. Party time!

January 4th, 2022, JP

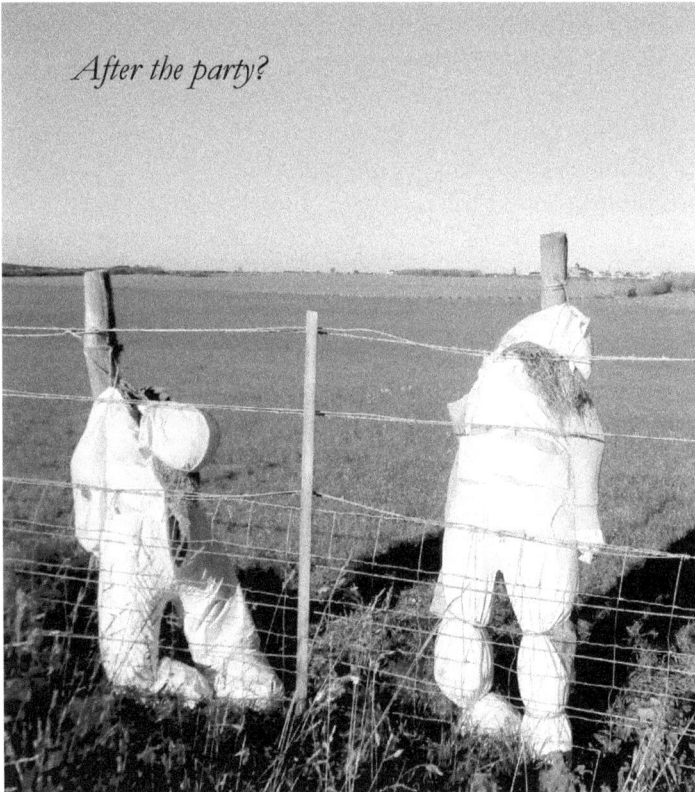

After the party?

Photo JP

Holding on to letting go

I've been counting the days since you died
I've been counting the hours
Counting the seconds
It's been a year now
I'm still holding on to letting go
Holding on to invisible hands
Looking up at an invisible smile
Looking down at what I won't let you fall into
The never ending darkness
But you're already gone
You've already fallen
You fell last year but I'm still holding on to letting go
Holding on to letting go
Holding on to your words replaying them in my head
Painting forget-me-nots over the words you said
Over your image over your smile and over your last breath
Holding on to letting go

April 28th, 2022, LF (age 14)

Eye on the Sparrow

This migrating bird
with oars for wings
has flown from home
only to be strung up
sprawled and floating

in mesh entanglement.
Calloused hands
come to loosen
pluck at strings
fold down wings,
clasped in a grip.

Leaving one hand free
to clamp on leg iron,
bird band, number plate
I.D. photo card,
label, fingerprint,
digital tracking device,
infrared paper trail,
biometric eye scan,
registration records
matching documents.

Detained before release
to where and what
lock down or lock up?

While we, free, desensitized
can barely wait to board
on planes flying streets
above the rest.

On Holy-days, returns and getaways.
Our journey safe and sound
can even be insured!

April 30th, 2022, AR

National Covid Memorial Wall, London. Photos: December 2022, JP
Other images of the wall on pages 117, 123, 158–160, and 189.
For information see page 158.

The Sea and Maria

The writer Maria Strani-Potts, a contributor to this volume, lost consciousness and drowned on the 7th of May 2022, while swimming in the sea at Dassia, in Corfu, the island where she was born in 1946. Jim Potts, who has contributed many poems and photos to this volume, met Maria in Corfu in 1967 and they were married in 1969. The sequence of poems which follows is a tribute to Maria, while also fitting the theme of mourning which runs through this volume. It has been possible to include some extracts from Maria's unpublished autobiography in which she writes of her deep love of the sea, and also the thoughts of her daughter on the first anniversary of Maria's death.

PRIKA

Her only dowry was the sea,
the best a man could have.
An empty chest. Her only dowry
the sea, the unspoilt sea!

circa 1970, JP

CORFU
*Many writers have wondered whether
Corfu is Homer's island of Scheria.*

What does it matter
if Odysseus swam here
and met Nausicaa on the shore?
Everything is in the sea,
the books can tell no more.

1968, JP

MARIA, SWIMMING

Her face,
a pale pink-primrose-and-orange-tinged oval
bobs like a buoy above the water's surface.
You can tell she's happy,
illuminated, all alone,
within her element, the wide blue sea.
The mountains frame her,
soft clouds backlight her
she makes few ripples as she goes.

See! See her out there, her face is blurred —
see how she smiles and brightly glows.

Summer 2020, JP

A CULTURAL MISTAKE

My wife is writing her memoirs.
She's exhausted by the effort.
"Give me a kiss," she says.
I bend down and kiss her forehead.

"You shouldn't kiss me on the forehead."
"Why not"? I ask (I can't reach her lips).
"Because we only kiss the *dead*
(the *dear departed*), on the forehead."

circa 2020, JP

MIROLOYI FOR MARIA — A LAMENT

The waves are weeping
like our children.
My hopes drowned with you
on May the Seventh.
I should have been beside you.
Instead, I took a walk,
as time was short
before our trip to town.
You couldn't resist
a quick morning dip.
On my return, I went up to change,
I'd called out I'd join you,
you'd waved, seemed happy in the water —
but before I was ready, before I'd come down,
you'd drowned. *You'd drowned.*
The sea had reclaimed you:
"You are ours again,
where Life began."

We tried long and hard
to bring you back.
So much water in lungs and stomach . . .
No sign of life, no pulse at all.
You lay there
like a stranded dolphin,
out of its element,
while I am doomed
to dry land without you.

I must try not to think —
as I do each day —

of that walnut box
in your native island,
while I am far away.

I'll have in mind
you in the sea,
the sea that loved you
but took you from me.

Late May 2022, JP

THE KEY

"Where did you leave the key?"
The last words I ever spoke to you.
I'm still haunted by your drowning.

We used to stretch washed sheets together.
It was easier for two to fold them.
That image keeps returning.

I used to reach the higher shelves
to put away the cups and plates.
"Tall men are the slaves of the short!"

I wish I could be your "slave" again.
I promise I'd never complain.

I'm searching for you — and you for me.
Where did you leave the key?

June 2022, JP

THE SEA

by
Dinos Christianopoulos

The sea is like love, like Eros:
you wade right in,
you never know if you'll come out.
How many youths have squandered lives
through fateful plunges or deadly dives,
risked cramps or currents, rips or rocks,
sharks or whirlpools,
medusas or men o' war?
Woe betide us if we should give up swimming
because half a dozen people drowned!
Woe betide us if we reject the sea,
for fear that she will swallow us.
The sea's like love, like Eros:
a thousand people take pleasure in it,
but one of us will pay the price.

free translation from the Greek, JP

LIFE ON LOAN — LIFE RECLAIMED

Answer me, Sea, why you took my love's life!
Answer me, Sea, why you stole my life's love.
I can't curse you again, you change every day.
I can't swim without thinking
        of that shore where she lay.

August 31st, 2022, JP

179

*Extracts from the "Epilogue" (November–December 2018)
to "Nomad, Migrant or Expatriate?"
an unpublished autobiography
by Maria Strani-Potts.*

The last ten years have been precious. I have settled down to write, to quilt and take stock of my life.

Living near the coast has been my salvation in England.

The Sea, the Sea: of all landscapes the seacoast is the one that feeds me, liberates me, inspires me, gives me joy. When swimming I leave my body behind. It is only my soul that goes through the water, through the waves. I want to swim to eternal space, to go on and on.

While I swim, I wonder why I didn't come into existence as a sea creature.

Life's journey has changed me beyond belief. When my time comes, I shall no longer be the person I was when I was an infant, Marigoula the redhead from Corfu. She died a long time ago.

When I left Corfu, I had hundreds of friends. I left them behind. I have remained close to my original friends. The ones who have died come back to my memory when I visit the Corfu cemetery. I see their graves next to our family grave in Garitsa. The Corfu cemetery is a good place to remember them all.

Many of my Corfiot friends have stayed on the island all their lives. They are at hand when I return. They are always welcoming and kind.

Fantina, Lena, Olga, Miranda, Maria, Anna, Ioanna, Xanthi have always been on the island waiting for me, ready to see me and to spend time with me each time I return.

In Greece I feel love, a Greek precious love. I feel included, taken care of. At times when I was young or feeling lonely, I would go out of the house and visit my friends: problem solved. When I was growing up, I was not brought up to spend time by myself. Greeks never do. We only feel comfortable in a crowd. "Parea" is such an important Greek word. In England I do not have a *parea*.

England educated me, changed me, but she failed to make me happy and comfortable in her fold. Greece will be with me until the day I die.

My mother's spirit — my guardian angel — sent me Jim. He opened the door in order for me to get in and see the world beyond Corfu. Because of Jim's job, I married not only him but Britain too. Who could have thought that a simple girl who'd learned English at a modest school in Corfu would be put in the position of representing Great Britain overseas?

In 2009 we made Poundbury, Dorchester, our home. I left my friends once again, left my world.

Dorchester's proximity to the sea, a sea that carried explorers from its shores to the very countries where I had been living and which I had come to know intimately, rejuvenates my sense of connection to these countries.

The sea is my connecting link. The sea makes me understand what I find alien when I gaze inland. The sea joins the patches of my life.

The daydreaming has come to an end. This is it! I have arrived where I was destined to be.

Perhaps I have not changed after all.

THE GLOBE AND THE PLAQUE

For her birthday she'd asked for a bedside globe,
a round metal map of the world.
She'd turn it round slowly, studying it closely,
retracing the places which she loved, where we'd lived,
where the children grew up,
where close friends had been made,
and plotting the oceans she'd swum in.

She didn't ask for the plaque,
which we'd had cast in bronze
to commemorate her life.
We had to send back the first casting,
on account of a terrible typo:
"Writer and Quitter" it read,
instead of "Writer and Quilter".

Maria was never a quitter!
There were so many countries
she still wanted to see —
and still more oceans
to swim in.

April 2023, JP

MARIA STRANI POTTS

1946 - 2022

WRITER AND QUILTER

Memorial plaque, Poundbury Cemetery

182

Thoughts of Maria's daughter
written down in the early hours of the morning
on the day of the one-year Memorial Service for Maria
held in the Greek Orthodox Cathedral
of the Holy Wisdom (Saint Sophia) in Washington, DC

Last (American) Mother's Day, I saw my mother dead, in the Corfu hospital morgue.

Since that day, I haven't been able to accept that she has gone.

I've held her in my arms, in my dreams, many times, and we've sunk together, with her red auburn hair entwined in mine, tangled strands floating above us, as I watch her helplessly, and her lungs fill with water. I try and pull her to the surface, but she keeps sinking . . . She says, "Go now, Nina, before you drown as well. Leave me here, in the sea." And she slips away, out of my arms.

I've had day-time visions of her appearing while I run a bath or cook a meal. I've been fully awake, and have seen her standing beside me, talking to me.

I dream we walk arm-in-arm, through the streets of Corfu, until we reach the front door of the apartment. She says, "You go upstairs, Nina, I can't come with you, you have to go now."

Even now, I sometimes reach for the phone to call her and then remember.

I've had days — too many to count — when I haven't been able to function. I've had to leave work in a rush, as if I were about to vomit, instead knowing a tidal wave of tears is about to hit. There have been times when it's gone on for days, and

I've not wanted to see or speak to anyone. Those days are fewer now, but not completely gone.

I have several friends (some here) who lost parents young. Or at the same time. Or who have lost siblings or children. Or who are facing their own protracted, painful death . . . I've known what grief is, and lost people. But I wish I'd really been there.

My own mother lost her mother when she was six.

My mother must have drowned in minutes. Her death certificate says "death by drowning", but I still wonder — almost daily — what happened, and what she felt in those final minutes and seconds. Did she say goodbye to us in her head? Did she try and call out?

My dearest friends say (and I almost believe it, I want to believe it) that she was lucky to have gone so fast, in the way that she did, in the sea that she loved.

And that we were lucky to have her in our lives for as long as we did.

A grief counsellor I saw briefly, said I'd develop "complex grief" if I didn't deal with it, and she warned me that it would likely cause permanent damage if I didn't talk to someone.

I don't really know what that means.

Perhaps her death was a trigger for an inner, different sort of crisis. Separated by the pandemic (two years! . . . at the end of which she kept asking me when I would come, and I kept saying, "I don't know mama, it depends on work"), separated by continents, separated by years at boarding school (ten!), separated from my own children during the pandemic. Maybe it made me go over all the mistakes I'd made and never had time (wanted?) to tell her. I wish I'd had time to say goodbye.

Of course, every experience of death and grief is personal, complex, complicated and deeply private . . . or very public.

Maybe other people wish you'd get over it or stop talking about it.

All I know, is that I am fundamentally changed forever. It's as if my DNA, my personality, everything about me, has been jumbled up in a machine-dryer and reconfigured.

And you never, ever, really know what people are going through.

Happy Mother's Day, Mama. I can't say those words, without wanting to tell you how I feel: lost without you, and very often like my heart's been torn out.

Sometimes I still feel angry about some of the fights we had.

But take that as a tribute to the person you are, and always will be, larger than life, exuberant, forceful, opinionated, sometimes maddening but motivated only by love. Your personality was huge.

Know that I want to be as strong as you were . . . and I won't waste a second of the life you gave me.

I am writing this at 2.30 a.m. in Washington on the 7th of May 2023. I just woke up suddenly, exactly one year (to the minute?) since you slipped away without warning. And I was too far away.

Nina-Maria Potts

CYPRESSES

The Cemetery.
Side by side two cypress trees.
You waiting for me.

August 31st, 2022, JP

*In the First
Cemetery of
Corfu, Garitsa,
Corfu Town*

ΜΑΡΙΑ ΣΤΡΑΝΗ ΡΟΤΤS
1946 - 2022
ΣΥΓΓΡΑΦΕΑΣ

Grave inscription in the First Cemetery

The left pocket of your leather jacket

It was things like this that touched my heart. Not the fact that you're gone or the fact that you used to live in this world with me. But the ways that you're still here.

I'm reminded of you when I think of how I opened the left pocket of your red leather jacket. I expected it to be empty but I found a small round object wrapped in plastic, rustling as I took it out. It was one of those slightly sour sweets you get with the bill. They always used to excite me when I was younger but now I'm seeing it and I'm thinking of you. I'm imagining the day you put it in your pocket and I'm imagining who you would have offered it to.

The next thing I found was a small piece of paper, about four inches folded twice. I opened it up to your handwriting. It was a shopping list. Quite hard to decipher but, from what I could understand, you wrote: mixed fruit, apricots, cereal and olive oil. Apricots were the only thing ticked off the list. Naturally, I wondered if you ever got the other things. I wondered if this was the last list you made and I wondered what you'd be thinking now that this list is in my hands. For a minute, I just stood there looking at the shopping list and the sweet and coming up with ideas, stories about them. These things made you so human and real that it felt as though you were still here with me.

September 19th, 2022, LF (age 14)

Counting

do you count the days away from me
do you count the crashes of the sea

do you count the words you never said
do you count the poems you never read

do you count the clouds in the sky
did you count my last unsaid goodbye

did you count the times I said I was sorry
did you count at all
did you even worry

I counted the leaves that fell in autumn
I counted the clothes you liked and bought them
I did this all because I live to love
I live to fall
To fall in love

October 15th, 2022, LF (age 14)

National Covid Memorial Wall, London. Photo: December 2022, JP
Other images of the wall on pages 117, 123, 158–60, and 174.
For information see page 158.

"Release people!"

Stop Zero Covid!
Holding blank sheets of paper —
protests in China.

November 28th, 2022, JP

Covid at last!

Almost three years now
and five doses of the vaccine
and Covid never touched me 'til today.

I felt a little odd all day.
Out Christmas shopping.
Not up to walking as briskly as I'd like.
Concentration well below par.
A bit of a cough, but nothing much
and I'd had that all week, or longer.

Back at home this evening
hot and cold by turns, and so
I did a Covid text, a "rapid antigen".

And sure enough — something
I'd never seen before — red lines
appeared beside both C and T.

C for Control (as in le Carré's spy tales)
has confused so many, thinking it was Covid.
And T? Toxic? Terror? Trauma? Terminal?
No, just Test. Not a very clever use of letters.
A plus sign instead of T would have been better
and anything at all in place of C.

A long deep hot bath before I went to bed.
Trying to get out, I fell back in.
A huge splash, no harm to me,
water all over the floor, though,
and my clothes that I had dumped there — soaked.

December 23rd, 2022, AH

Marx on surplus value: the case of dairy farming

Early on in the pandemic
all that talk of "herd immunity". . .

It's only now it strikes me
almost three years later
how insulting that really was . . .

And how revealing! . . . WE —
the general population —
are the HERD which THEY —
our amateur politicians — MILK
for the benefit of THEIR
professional colleagues — RICH
business men and women, boards

of directors who get FAT
on the product of our grazing
and chewing cud for thirty,
forty, fifty hours a week . . .

More than fifty for many
in the NHS these past three years —
overworked, distressed and underpaid . . .

But then the government
has no more money. Don't ASK
where it's gone. Don't even MENTION
Lady Mone on the sundeck of her yacht . . .
or at a ski resort, six thousand pounds a night . . .

Give me hereditary peers any day
harmlessly snoozing on their benches in the Lords.

December 24th, 2022, AH

Covid, Day 2

Not much to report.
Between two and four a.m.
night-sweats reduced my temperature
almost to normal.

Around six a.m., in bed still,
the poem about herd immunity
and dairy farming came to me.
I took it down, as if from
dictation, on my bedside pad —

"A4 ruled and margin" —
like me ruled by Covid
with a margin in which
to function normally.

But definitely not feeling A4,
never mind A1, or "in the pink" . . .   "

(About a hundred years
ago, when she was young,
my mother's family had
a live-in housemaid, who,
when on her annual holiday —
a week in some boarding house
in Blackpool, Bridlington or Scarb'rough —
would send back a picture postcard,
the message always the same:
"Hope this finds you A1
as it leaves me in the pink.
Love Violet.")

Got up late. The day passed
in a blur. In the afternoon
tried to do some typing, but
brain-to-hand co-ordination
gone to pot. Almost every word
came out with at least one pair
of reversed letters and other
letters that just did not belong.

A film on TV in the evening.
No recollection now of what it was.

December 24th, 2022, AH

Covid, Day 3 (Xmas Day)

Night-sweats for longer this time.
From one to five a.m. Up though
for breakfast at the normal time.

After opening presents — to each other
and those dropped off before
by friends and family, I spent
the day working at my desk.
translating French. Typing
still a mess, but having something
to occupy and stretch my mind
allowed me, when not wracked
by coughing or having to mop
my freely streaming nose, to ignore
my body's aches and tightnesses.

At the end of the afternoon
I thought that I'd feel better
for another long hot bath.

At first I did, just lying there.
Getting out was still a struggle,
although I didn't fall back in
this time and make a splash.

Once out, feeling light-headed,
sat down, still wet, on the toilet,
lid down, towel round my shoulders.

What happened next I'm really
not quite sure — passed out,
or fell asleep, it's much the same.

Nor how long it was before
I found myself folded up,
foetal position, on the floor
unable to move — brain
out of contact with my muscles,
head very sore — the right side
it seems had met the bath panel,
the bony ridge above the eyes
had had a violent disagreement
with the glass-topped bathroom scales.

Help came, responding to the noise
I suppose, and eventually
I managed to sit up. Then stand,
and was conducted up to bed,
given a bucket to pee in
and forbidden to go down
to the bathroom in the night
for fear of further falls.

December 25th, 2022, AH

Covid, Day 6

Nothing new for me today
(or in the last two days)
except that this evening
I lost my sense of taste
and sense of smell.

I'd made myself bacon
and eggs for supper. The bacon

just tasted salty, and the eggs
had no taste at all, my glass
of wine like dirty water.

I tried sniffing various things
to no effect. Not even
half an onion. I found it
in the fridge wrapped in clingfilm,
unwrapped it, sniffed it hard
but there was nothing there at all
and even my eyes didn't water.

I hope it won't last long —
a nasty taste — ! — of how much pleasure
would have gone from life
if food lost all its flavour.

My wife has got it now.
At first, for her, it was
a sleeping sickness — thirty
hours in thirty six quite out of it.
Only felt well enough to test
this evening. Positive.

Nights we lie in separate
adjacent rooms, coughing
each other out of sleep
through the partition wall.

December 28th, 2022, AH

Happy Birthday, Mr C

Quite recent your third birthday must have been,
though the exact date of your birth remains —
maybe always will remain — a Chinese puzzle.

I've written quite a lot about you, Covid,
but never said you were to blame, remember?

It never was your choice to be a virus.
It never was my choice to be a human.

Yours is a miserable life, I'd say.
Even your status as a living organism
remains a matter of debate for us.

But each and every human is another world
ready and waiting for you to colonise.

Yet none of your new worlds can serve you long.
Either your growing numbers overwhelm, destroy it,
or else it recovers, destroying most of you.

In either case a few of you escape —
or, rather, a few million, I should say —
escape into the hostile air, where time
is limited for you to find your next new world.

And time for you moves so much faster than for us.
"A thousand of *your* ages in *our* sight
are like an evening gone." And yet, perhaps,
in our slow way, we're really just like you.

So successful have we at last become

in our one world, have multiplied so fast
that we're destroying our own habitat, our home.

And some of the more ingenious idiots
amongst us say that we must colonise the moon,
or Mars, that to survive we must (or Musk)
become "an interplanetary species".

Ere long, eh, Elon? Meanwhile we'll
just keep on twittering.

But you,
dear Mr C, are, I think, far better
at adapting to new worlds than we
could ever even, Elon, hope to be.

January 4th, 2023, AH

Covid, Day 16

Tested negative at last.
Yesterday the red T-line was feint,
today not there at all, just C.

Dear Mr C (the other C),
you have been kind to me, left me
unharmed it seems, for now. A nasty
cough remains, but not for long, I hope.

Has the residue of my protracted
international vaccine cocktail —two parts
Vaxzevria by AstraZeneca AB

(Aktiebolag), three parts Comimaty
by Biontech Manufacturing GmbH
(Gesellschaft mit beschränkter Haftung) —
has it made me, in the good old
gov-dot-uk way, a "hostile
environment" for immigrants like you?

. . . Limited liability all round,
you understand. No one to blame.

January 7th, 2023, AH

Home-made poster in a window in Palatine Road, London N16.
Photo: October 6th, 2023, AH, by permission of the house owners.

Nothing News To Say

What a relief the media landscape went from Brexit to pestilence. Just when we were bored to tears along came Covid "on the road map" to frighten us to death.

Out went "Brexit means Brexit" in came oft repeated terms and turns of fashionable words. To name a few old and new, in no particular order:

no pressure, no worries, once in a generation, prorogue parliament, new normal, platform, diss, passed (not passed away!), supply chains, surreal, absolutely, take to the next level, hammered, AirBnB, backlog, too much information, fake news, chime, living wage, drill down into, aspirational, impact, own it, tanking, pass the buck, pandemic, WiFi, nuanced, capacity, weapons of mass destruction, going forward, Netflix, PPE, furlough, toxic, stay-cation, zooming, lockdown, asymptomatic, algorithm, world class, living on the edge, distancing, compliance, self-isolating, track and trace, quantitative easing, targets, bubble, spam, Vaxx and jabs, living the dream, snowflake, damp squib, process (vb.), food banks, top down, bottom up, levelling up, pants, suck it up, brain fog, Long Covid, in lock-step, connect the dots, lose the will to live, eye-watering, getting ahead of the curve, pushback, keeping schtum, blue-sky thinking, no brainer, crowd funding, woke, crusties, lots of laughs (LOL), cloud, static, what's that about? magic money tree, austerity, life-changing, hybrid, spiking, second wave, pronoun, perfect storm, bottom line, meltdown, balanced, streaming, spotify, tweet, crypto currency, neuro-divergent, loopholes, bricking it, corona, omicron, new variants, backlog, 21st Century Woman, climate change, trolls, Just Stop Oil, oven-ready, sound bar, get your knickers in a twist, lose your wig, deep pockets, going viral, vrooom, cancel culture, couch potato, push-back, non-dom, virtual, glass ceiling, asylum seeker, back to better, cloud, factor in, fake news, awesome, Net Zero, democracy, cyber, vector, log-in, doxx, OFSTED, carbon footprint, selfie, taking back control, windfall, conspicuous consumption, diversity, marginalized, trending, bespoke, emoji, Black Lives Matter, burning issue, wing-it, blue-light services, Arctic Storm, elephant in the room . . .

New memes keep coming. There's no escaping the Urban Dictionary of broadcast mimicked buzzwords like so many bees playing kazoos in the poppies.

Some phrases "faze" or fade away in phases, so thin they've lost their origin. Others circle back like "Brexit". How will protocol be defined? Protocol: a blank page at the beginning or end of a book.

January 18th, 2023, AR

INDEX TO POEMS, PROSE AND PICTURES
BY CONTRIBUTOR

KEY TO CONTRIBUTORS

Page numbers in upright characters indicate poems or prose pieces; those in italic type, images; page ranges in bold type are used only for the two memorial tributes to contributors Faysal Mikdadi and Maria Strani-Potts. Where images are integral to the poems they accompany and were provided by the author of the poem in question, they are not indexed separately from the poem. Names in italics are not those of contributors but of other authors whose work is quoted or translated.

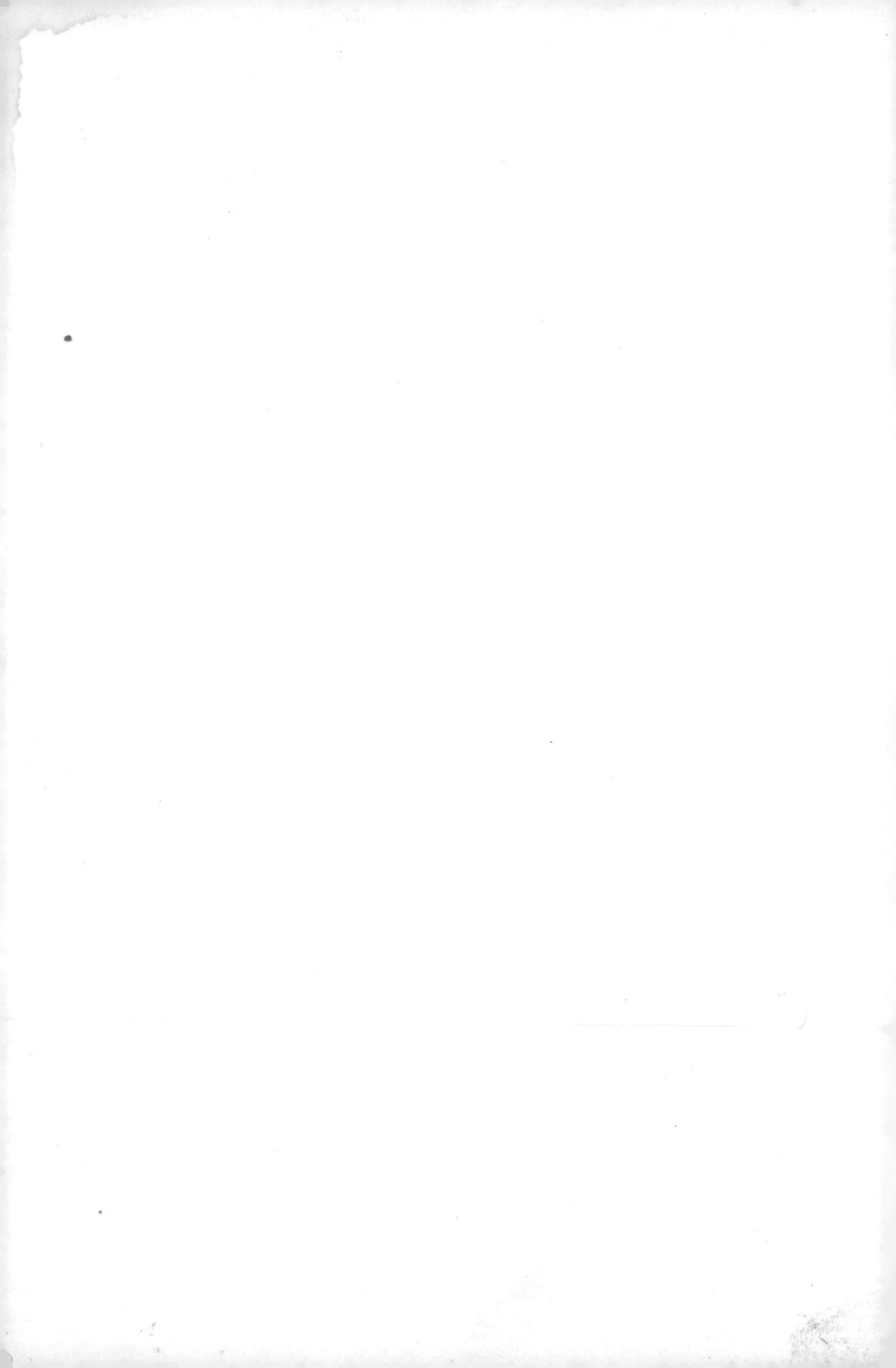